DIRTY DEVIL

A J.J. GRAVES MYSTERY

LILIANA HART

ALSO BY LILIANA HART

JJ Graves Mystery Series

Dirty Little Secrets

A Dirty Shame

Dirty Rotten Scoundrel

Down and Dirty

Dirty Deeds

Dirty Laundry

Dirty Money

A Dirty Job

Dirty Devil

Playing Dirty

The MacKenzies of Montana

Dane's Return

Thomas's Vow

Riley's Sanctuary

Cooper's Promise

Grant's Christmas Wish

Jayden's Hope

The MacKenzies Boxset

MacKenzie Security Series

Seduction and Sapphires

Shadows and Silk

Secrets and Satin

Sins and Scarlet Lace

Sizzle

Crave

Scorch

MacKenzie Security Omnibus 1

MacKenzie Security Omnibus 2

Lawmen of Surrender (MacKenzies-1001 Dark Nights)

1001 Dark Nights: Captured in Surrender

1001 Dark Nights: The Promise of Surrender

1001 Dark Nights: Sweet Surrender

1001 Dark Nights: Dawn of Surrender

The MacKenzie World (read in any order)

Trouble Maker

Bullet Proof

Deep Trouble

Delta Rescue

Desire and Ice

Rush

Spies and Stilettos

Wicked Hot

Hot Witness

Avenged

Never Surrender

Addison Holmes Mystery Series

Whiskey Rebellion

Whiskey Sour

Whiskey For Breakfast

Whiskey, You're The Devil

Whiskey on the Rocks

Whiskey Tango Foxtrot

Whiskey and Gunpowder

The Gravediggers

The Darkest Corner

Gone to Dust

Say No More

Stand Alone Titles

Breath of Fire

Kill Shot

Catch Me If You Can

All About Eve

Paradise Disguised

Island Home

The Witching Hour

Books by Liliana Hart and Scott Silverii

The Harley and Davidson Mystery Series

The Farmer's Slaughter

A Tisket a Casket

I Saw Mommy Killing Santa Claus

Get Your Murder Running

Deceased and Desist

Malice In Wonderland

Tequila Mockingbird

Gone With the Sin

Published by 7th Press
Dallas, TX 75115

To my readers—may you find peace, joy and escape between the pages of a book.

ACKNOWLEDGMENTS

A huge thanks to my editors, Imogen Howson and Anne Welch, and my cover designers, Damon Freeman and Dar Albert.

And always, thank you, Scott. You're the best partner, husband, sounding board, and police consultant a woman could ask for.

Any mistakes are mine alone.

PROLOGUE

JOHN DONNELLY LIKED A GOOD DRINK. AND IF THE drink was whiskey, even better.

The Judge's Chamber was barely half full on a Wednesday night, but it was the only place in King George County to get a decent drink without being hassled. And boy, did he deserve a drink after the day he'd had.

The plaintiff had crumbled beautifully on the stand. And if John had a soul, the tears she'd shed would have bothered him. But he'd sold his soul a long time ago. His client was guilty as hell, but it was never about guilt or innocence—lies or truth. It wasn't even about the victim or the accused.

It was about the game.

It was the skill, the intelligence, and the outmaneuvering of his opponent that made his blood sing. He'd learned over his thirty-plus years in law that the truth rarely mattered. Money, power, cunning… that's what separated the men from the boys.

It didn't bother him that he was drinking alone. It was par for the course. He liked the solitude and the silence before going home to Kimmie, where Lord knew she'd talk him to death about whatever it was she did all day. He found it best to go into conversations with her with his brain numb.

The Judge's Chamber was the best the county had to offer. It was considered high class among the locals, despite the scratched hardwood floors and the eclectic décor—from antlers of various sizes and species to a framed replica of the Constitution and a moth-eaten wig supposedly worn by Charles Henry, who was one of King George's first judges—though he was eventually hanged for treason. There was history and tradition here, and Virginians loved both.

John sat in his usual place at the end of the long mahogany bar, so he could see everyone coming in and going out. There'd been times in his career he'd been threatened, and sometimes the victims he'd trampled wanted to confront him or try to guilt him into doing the right thing. He snorted a laugh into his tumbler. His own mother couldn't have guilted him into doing the right thing unless the price was right.

Lightning flashed bright white through the distorted glass in the windows, but no one paid much attention. Weather couldn't chase away the regulars who came to drown their pain.

Officers Mahoney, Durrant, Cole, and Smith were huddled together at a corner table, laughing at whatever inside joke had been shared, their empty bottles multiplying with impressive speed. They were off duty, but there was no question they were cops. Cops always stuck together, and they didn't welcome outsiders crashing their party. That particular crew had been in more frequently since they'd lost one of their own several months back.

Junie Ward sat in her regular spot, staring out the window and nursing a Jack and Coke, her worn boots propped up on the chair across from her. She'd never been right in the head after her family had been killed when a bridge collapsed on their car. She'd gotten a huge settlement, but you'd never know it by looking at her. Most people who didn't know better thought she was homeless. She hadn't stepped foot in a car since the accident, so she'd shuffle around town or stand on the edge of the bridge looking out over the river for hours at a time. He'd never given it much thought as to how she'd get home from the bar, especially with the weather as bad as it was. But clearly, she managed somehow.

He shrugged Junie off as his gaze passed over a couple he'd never seen before having a whispered argument. They didn't look like locals. They looked city polished, so they were either lost, trying to wait out the storm, or visiting someone.

"I heard you killed it today in court," Mike Costello said, polishing a glass from behind the bar.

Mike was a decent guy. He was short and built like a bull, his neck so thick there probably wasn't a button-down shirt in creation that would fit him. His dark hair was thinning on top, but he kept it cropped so close to his head it hardly mattered. With the hair he lacked on top of his head, it was more than made up for on the rest of his body. His arms were covered in dark wiry hair, and a small tuft sprouted from the top of his T-shirt.

"It was a slam dunk," John said, pushing his glass back across the bar for a refill. "My client was cleared of all charges, I get a big fat check, and Kimmie and I are headed to Aruba to celebrate in a few days. She's been bugging me for months to take a vacation."

"Didn't Kimmie just get back from Paris?"

John rolled his eyes. "I didn't say *she* needed a vacation. I said she's been begging me to take one. She likes to take her shopping trips, but she says it doesn't count as a vacation. Go figure on that one."

"Ah, the logic of a woman," Mike said, his grin showing a chipped front tooth. "I could be wrong, but I don't think you hooked up with her for her brains."

John snorted again. "Lord, isn't that the truth. The only place that woman is useful is in a mall or in bed. But when I send her on her trips, it keeps her out of my hair. And it makes her happy. When she's happy, then she keeps me happy. Everybody wins."

"Spoken like a man who learned something from his divorces," Mike said, chuckling.

John toasted his friend in acknowledgment. "Ah, marriage, the most expensive life sentence on the planet."

"Only when they find out you're spending all the money on your sidepiece."

John smiled. His divorces had been no secret. In fact, his second divorce had made quite a splash across the media. Christine had been right pissed to find out he'd been cheating on her, and she'd packed up her stuff and the kids, and then set his stuff on fire on the front lawn on her way out. He hadn't been quite as successful back then as he was now. It was all water under the bridge, but the alimony and child support had still stung.

"Life without danger isn't a life worth living," John said.

He and Mike had started their careers around the same time, though Mike was a good ten years younger than he was. He'd never really had friends, but if there was anyone he'd call in a pinch it would be Mike. Law and order. They'd both believed in it once upon a time. He remembered the good old days, when they'd been naïve enough to think they could help victims and clean up the city, though John had been young and naïve at the DA's office and Mike had been a patrolman working the streets.

But dreams changed.

Mike hadn't planned on taking a bullet to the knee after a dozen years on the job. It was only good luck he hadn't eaten a bullet to escape his misery. Instead, he'd cashed out his pension to buy land and open a bar in the middle of nowhere. It had turned out to be a good business decision, because developers had come in to buy up a bunch of the land and paid him a fortune for it. Now there were rows of tract houses and a strip mall a couple miles down the road, and Mike was loaded.

John could sympathize with the temptation to play Russian roulette with one's life—to wonder if everyone would be better off without you—or if death could really chase away the pain. He'd thought about it himself a time or two. But when it came down to it, he was just too selfish. He had no interest in finding out what waited for him in the great beyond. He enjoyed the alcohol and the women and his work. He couldn't imagine there was much better for him in the afterlife.

This life was the only one he could control. And when things got hard, the alcohol did a pretty good job of numbing the things he didn't want to think about. It just so happened he'd picked the right profession. Criminals were like cockroaches, and he'd learned fast that it was better to look out for himself and line his pockets than have some altruistic notion of serving the greater good.

He didn't care what anyone said, money made everything better. His wives had certainly thought so over the decade or so he'd been married to each of them. He couldn't even blame them for taking the kids and moving on with their lives. They'd ended up buying houses next door to each other on a cul-de-sac so the kids could all stay close.

And now he had Kimmie. She was twenty-two, younger than his four children, and built like a pinup. She didn't care what he looked like, what hours he worked, or what he wanted her to do in the bedroom, as long as she had access to his credit cards.

A crack of thunder boomed loud enough to shake the rafters, and conversations died down as the lights dimmed briefly before coming back to full brightness. The rain was getting steadily worse, and if the color of the sky was anything to go by, all hell was about to break loose.

He pushed his empty glass back across the bar and tossed down a fifty. He was feeling generous, especially since Mike always made sure his glass stayed full.

"You heading out?" Mike asked, wiping down the other end of the bar.

"Weather is getting worse," he said, struggling into the overcoat he'd placed on the seat next to him.

"Tell me about it," Mike said. "I'm shutting down before too long. Chance of tornadoes in the area tonight. Things are looking real bad."

"Sounds like a good night to stay in," John said, waggling his eyebrows. "You got any of that fancy bubbly back there? Kimmie doesn't know it yet, but she's going to want to celebrate my big win. I bought her a little black number I've been waiting to give her for a special occasion."

"Careful, man," Mike said, grinning. "That girl is going to give you a heart attack."

He shrugged. "There are worse ways to die."

"The champagne will set you back two hundred," Mike said. "I've got a couple of bottles left."

"I'll take them both," John said, opening up his wallet and counting out the cash.

Mike raised his brows. "That little black number must be worth it."

John smiled and it took him two attempts to put his wallet in his coat pocket. He needed to get back in the gym. This last case had taken it out of him. Appearances were important, and he could admit he'd put on a few extra pounds around the middle over the last couple of months. A little exercise was just the ticket. What the hell did his doctor know, anyway? His health was just fine.

"Take my advice, Mikey, and find you a young one," he said. "They're worth every penny, and you'll die a happy man."

"I'm pretty sure Cathy would be the only one who was happy while she was murdering me," Mike said, chuckling. "And knowing Cathy, it would be painful."

John shrugged philosophically. He figured Mike and Cathy had been married going on thirty years now. He wasn't jealous. Sometimes he wondered what his life would have been like if he'd been a better husband and father, but he tried not to have regrets. He'd accepted his life, and it was what it was. He was happy. And when Kimmie was gone—as she inevitably would be once she realized he was serious about never getting married again—then he'd replace her with whatever Tiffany or Brittany or Jackie was waiting in line to warm his bed.

"Here you go," Mike said, coming out of the back room and handing him the two bottles. Then he lowered his voice and nodded at the group of cops in the corner. "Be careful as you pass Broken Bow Road. They've got a speed trap set up because people keep running the stop sign."

John grunted in acknowledgment. "I'll take my chances. I've never met a cop who would leave the warmth of his car and get out in the rain because someone ran a stop sign."

"You know Jack Lawson doesn't put up with any of that stuff," Mike said.

His lips tightened in annoyance. The sheriff wasn't someone who could be bought off. Political pressure could be applied if it came down to it, of course, but even he knew it'd be foolish to wave a red flag in front of Jack Lawson. It was a crying shame, because with Lawson—and Lawson's money—in his pocket, they could've run the whole county and most of the state.

"Thanks for the drink," John said.

He made his way past the group of cops, feeling their eyes on him as he pushed the swinging door open and walked into the vestibule. The temperature immediately dropped, but the whiskey was still warming his blood so he didn't bother trying to button his coat.

The rain wasn't going to let up anytime soon, so he tightened his grip on the champagne bottles and pushed open the outer door. The wind blew fiercely, causing him to stumble backward, and cold rain slashed across his face. Water dripped into his eyes, and slid down the neck of his coat, snaking down his back.

He swore and hurried his steps toward the little red Porsche he'd bought for his last birthday. At least he'd had the sense to park near the door. Not that it did much good. He could barely see a foot in front of his face. It was as if all the color had been sucked out of everything around him, and he was surrounded by a black-and-white movie. Except for the sky. It was greenish in hue and reminded him of the bruises that had covered the woman who'd testified against his client earlier that day.

His teeth chattered, and he shoved one of the champagne bottles under his arm so he could reach for the keys in his pocket. He hit the unlock button and saw his lights flash, and then the champagne bottle slipped out from under his arm and he heard the shatter of glass.

"Damn."

His reflexes weren't as swift as they normally were, and he juggled his keys and the other bottle ungracefully, managing to save the last bottle, but not the keys.

He swore, looking at the keys sitting atop the glittering shards of glass, and went unsteadily to one knee. He was already soaked to the skin, so a little more didn't matter. He picked gingerly through the glass for his keys, and didn't even feel the slice across his finger as he picked them up.

This wasn't how he'd envisioned his night going. John hurriedly made his way toward the car, no longer in the mood to crack open the remaining bottle of champagne, or even see Kimmie in the little black number for that matter. He wanted a hot shower and another glass of whiskey, not necessarily in that order.

It was a good half hour drive home, maybe longer with the weather the way it was. He had half a mind to stop at the little motel in Bloody Mary since it was closer. He wasn't fit for company, and his mood would have Kimmie holding out on him for a week.

He jerked the door of the Porsche open and tossed the champagne bottle on the passenger seat. He turned to slide in when he caught a flash of movement from the corner of his eye. The blow crashed through his skull, and he felt something break inside him. Then again. By the third blow he felt nothing at all.

1

I WAS A TRAITOR.

I knew it deep down in the pit of my soul, and the brief flash of guilt took me by surprise. But after a moment of self-evaluation, I decided I didn't care all that much.

"I'll take a dozen glazed, and two coffees to go," I said to the perky girl behind the counter. "And I'll take a vanilla crème and a Nutella-filled too. But put them in a separate bag."

My name is J.J. Graves, and I'm the coroner for King George County, Virginia. During my tenure, I'd spent more than my fair share of time on the news due to the fact that I was married to the sheriff, so I was fairly well known in the community. My celebrity status had recently extended to state news, and had even been picked up by the big stations in D.C.

I think it's because small, country crimes have a certain flair about them that the big city doesn't have to offer. I don't know if it's because people in the country have more time to be creative, that they might have more tools at their disposal, or that they're just plain crazy, but I've had some interesting cases come across my slab the last couple of years.

I'm not ashamed to say the specialty donuts were just for me. If I put them in the box with the others the wolves would descend and I'd be left with nothing. I knew this from experience. Some lessons were hard learned.

I heard the judgmental cluck of a tongue behind me, but I didn't turn around. I was on a mission to get in and out of Lady Jane's Donuts without too many people seeing me. A mission I'd clearly failed at considering the number of times I'd frequented the shop.

"Sure thing, Doc," the girl said. "Here's your number. You can wait over there."

I took the ticket and felt the flush creep over the back of my neck. There were no secrets in Bloody Mary. I knew my traitorous actions had already been reported to Tom Daly at the Donut Palace several days ago. But the Donut Palace didn't have pastries that melted like hot sugar across the tongue and made my eyes roll back in my head. I didn't want to tell Jack, but Lady Jane's Donuts came a very close second to sex.

There were three people waiting for orders in front of me, and there was a line that went clear out the door behind me. Lady Jane's would be completely sold out of that morning's fare within the hour. I knew this from experience because I'd showed up twice a little after eight and they'd already put out the closed sign. The difficult acquisition of said donuts made them all the more appealing. Which was why everyone in King George County was schlepping their way to Bloody Mary before the crack of dawn to stand in line, myself included.

"They'll go straight to your hips," Eileen Buckle said, clutching her handbag in front of her. "You won't keep that young stud of a husband with donuts on your thighs."

"How is Arthur?" I asked her, my smile polite. Arthur Buckle weighed four hundred pounds on a good day. I dreaded the day I'd have to bury him. Good help was hard to find. Or at least the kind of help that could put four hundred pounds in the ground with ease.

Her lips pursed like she'd bitten something sour, and she had the decency to look the other way. To my recollection, Eileen had been a sourpuss for as long as I'd known her.

There was a snort of laughter from behind Eileen and I turned to see the source. I hadn't really paid attention to the other traitors. I was too focused on my own betrayal. I'd learned over the past couple of

But my phone ringing in my coat pocket threw a wrench in my coordination.

I carefully put the cups in the center console and the donuts on the passenger seat before digging for the phone. It was Jack. A thrill of pleasure went through me at the sight of his picture on my screen. He'd left before I'd woken that morning. We'd been through a lot together, including the death hotel a few weeks back that Chuck Grable had mentioned.

"Hey," I said, smiling as I got into the car and closed the door behind me. There was a car heading toward me and a car behind me, and they were going to fight to the death for the parking spot I was about to vacate.

"Hey, yourself," he said. "Let me guess. Lady Jane's?"

I narrowed my eyes and scanned the line of people outside the shop. I spotted Betsy Clement about halfway down the block, seemingly focused on the rhinestone boots and fringed vest in the window of the boutique Western wear shop, but I knew she was using the reflection to watch me. The snitch.

Betsy was Jack's secretary, and she'd held the position of secretary to the sheriff for almost forty years. She was loyal to the position, knew everything about everyone, and there was no telling how many secrets she'd take to her grave when the time came.

"Yeah, so?" I asked. "Maybe you need to tell Betsy that snitches get stiches."

Jack barked out a laugh and said, "Yeah, I'm sure that would go over well. Word has it the Donut Palace has lost so much business Tom is thinking about closing up shop."

I felt bad about that. Really, I did. Tom was a good guy. "He's just got to reinvent himself. Things will die down once the newness of Lady Jane's wears off, and he'll be just fine. Maybe he should start opening at night. How many times have I wanted a midnight donut, but there was no way to get one?"

"More times than I can count," Jack said, patiently. "I'll make sure to pass on your idea to him."

"It's just that Lady Jane's Donuts are delicious," I said. "I mean, Tom's donuts were good, and you don't know what you're missing if that's the status quo. But then I had one of Lady Jane's and I realized there's a whole world I've been missing out on. It's an out-of-body experience. Almost sexual."

I heard Jack try to cover a laugh, but I wasn't offended. Jack didn't love food the way I did. He was an incredible chef, which was a crying shame because he rarely partook of his creations. He liked to cook for others' enjoyment, most specifically, mine. But Jack's body was a temple, and I'd learned to stop feeling guilty because my diet consisted of carbs and coffee and his consisted of weird greens and grasses I'd seen animals eat at the zoo.

But I couldn't really complain about the results. Most of the men I knew who were Jack's age had a keg instead of a six-pack. Jack's body was rock hard in all the right places, and if wheatgrass was what it took to keep a chiseled physique, then who was I to stop him?

"Sexual?" he asked. "Sounds like we need to do a test."

I'd been in the process of pulling the Suburban into the street between an opening of cars, but his suggestion had me slamming on the brakes. I managed to keep the donuts from sliding to the floor and I waved at the car that had felt it necessary to honk. I think I might have blacked out for a second. The thought of Lady Jane's Donuts and sex with Jack in some kind of American Ninja Warrior competition where I was the prize was now in the number one spot on my bucket list.

"Yes," I said, enthusiastically. "A test. That's exactly what we need to do. I can be at the house in fifteen minutes."

Jack laughed again, and I was already formulating what I'd say to my receptionist as far as why I'd failed to bring donuts into the office and why I would be late, but Jack burst my bubble.

"We'll have to reschedule for another day," he said. "Maybe you could see what dates Betsy has available in my calendar."

"I know lots of ways to kill a man without getting caught," I said, maneuvering my way between the cars inching closer to my spot. I finagled my way out and headed to the light at the end of the street. The timing was just right for the green light, so I made a left and headed toward the funeral home.

"You know it turns me on when you say things like that," he said.

"That's weird. Maybe keep that one to yourself."

I put Jack on speaker and then dug into the little white bag that had my special treats inside. I had just enough time to finish them both off before I pulled into the carport at the funeral home. Timing was everything. The first bite into Nutella-filled pastry had me making a sound I knew Jack recognized.

"Before you get too deep into your experience," he said. "I need you to head out to County Road 642."

I thought for a minute and said, "I have no idea where that is. And why do you need me?"

"We got a report early this morning of a body. I think I'll wait to give you any details and let you see it for yourself."

"Interesting," I said, pulling to the side of the road to see if my GPS brought up County Road 642. "But maybe lead with the whole body thing next time instead of getting me worked up over donuts and sex."

"Noted," he said. "I didn't want to ruin your breakfast."

"Nothing can ruin my breakfast."

2

THE LAST COUPLE OF DAYS HAD BEEN BRUTAL. THE storms had brought crazy wind, hail, and a couple of tornadoes that had touched down and wreaked a path of destruction across several miles of land. There'd been power outages all over the state, so the electric company was working around the clock to get everyone back up and running. There'd been several homes, cars, and other property damaged, keeping Jack and the other officers doing welfare checks, unblocking roadways, and dealing with the numerous other problems that came with natural disasters.

I'd really only seen Jack in passing the last couple of days. He came in long after I fell asleep, and was up and gone before my alarm went off. And now, on top of everything else, we had a body to deal with.

I hadn't driven every inch of the county like Jack had, so I wasn't familiar with Broken Bow Road.

But it came up on my GPS, which was more than I could say for the county road where the body had been found.

Potholes were filled with mud and water, and I could see several spots where trees and limbs that had fallen in the road had been dragged into ditches. I followed the muddy tire tracks onto a single-lane gravel road and crossed my fingers I was in the right place. I drove almost a mile, past nothing but trees, before the space opened up into open farmland.

There was an old white house with a wraparound porch on the right, and there was a big red barn behind it. But all the first responder vehicles were parked farther down the road on the opposite side.

It was a pretty spot, and fields of wheat-colored grass blew gently with the breeze. There was a slight incline as I continued up the road until the landscape stopped as it dropped off into the Potomac.

But it was the sight of the body that took my breath away. He—I assumed it was a he based on his size—was propped up on a scarecrow pole, his arms splayed wide and his head covered by a big straw-brimmed hat. I couldn't see the details, but the front of him was covered in blood. The irritated vultures circling above made me wince. There was no telling what was left of the body. Scavengers made forensics work difficult, especially if there were missing organs that could be vital to the case.

There weren't many cops on the scene. Just a handful—Cole, Riley, Hops, Walters, and Martinez. Resources were stretched thin with everything that had been going on with the storms. Shoulders were slumped, and brows were furrowed—exhaustion. It wasn't a posture I was used to seeing. I looked around, but didn't see Jack anywhere.

I left the keys in the ignition and put the donuts in the back seat for protection before I got out onto soggy ground. My boots sunk into mud and I swore as I remembered I was wearing my nice ones, but it was too late to save them now. They squelched with every step as I made my way to the back of the Suburban. I hit the button for the liftgate and sat on the cargo space so I could take my shoes off and start the process of getting suited up.

I pulled on coveralls and my old rain boots and waited to stand before I zipped up the front of the coveralls. It was a cool morning, but the sun shone bright in a cloudless sky, and a light sheen of sweat covered my skin. I dug in my bag for something to pull my hair back with and saw the shadow creep over my shoulder.

"So," I said, knowing it was Jack before I turned to look at him. "This seems different."

"It's a new one for me too," he said. "You think you've seen everything, and then someone takes things to a new level."

that were so clear we could live and breathe the life of the victim.

"Cotton said there wasn't anything in the field but the old scarecrow when he went to bed last night. He did a final check in the barn around eight o'clock and then headed inside. So sometime between eight and five this morning the body was dumped out here. This definitely wasn't the kill site."

"No," I agreed. I didn't see any large pools of blood or spatter. Just what covered the front of the victim.

"He's well dressed," Jack said. "That's not a cheap suit. His shirt is tailored. But the suit jacket is missing."

"That's not all that's missing," I said.

"Yeah," Jack said, his lips pressed into a thin line. "He's been gutted. But they buttoned his shirt back after they did it. Maybe the killer wanted to give the vultures a head start at destroying evidence."

"It's sick," I said. "He was already dead when they put him up here. Why would they go to the added trouble of disemboweling him and then buttoning his shirt back to hold in his intestines? Not that it worked very well."

The vultures had picked at the delicate tissue until the entrails had spilled out on the ground and his shirt was held together by one straining button.

"You said it," he said. "They're sick. But I think there's a message here. It's like you said, why would someone go to the added trouble when they've already committed the murder? You've got a man who's got money, not only in his clothes, but look at his hands. He gets manicures."

"His fingers have all been broken," I said, noting the swollen and crooked joints. "Someone wants to send a very strong message." Then I looked at Jack. "You think the message is for us?"

"Maybe," he said. "Too soon to tell. We'll know more once we get an identification."

"You really think someone my size could get him up there? That just one person could do this?"

Jack squatted down and moved some of the tall grass so I could see where the pole was driven into the ground.

"One person could do it," he said. "They'd have to be familiar with this farm, and this particular setup, but it can be done. The owner of the farm has these scarecrow posts in every field. They're built like a cross, and pretty sturdy pieces of metal. There's already a posthole dug for the pipe, so all the killer would have to do is take it out of the hole and lay it down flat. From there, it'd be easy to tie the victim down and use leverage to push the pipe back down into the hole."

"Have y'all finished photographing?" I asked.

"All done," he said. "Just waiting on you before we take him down."

I normally brought my camera to crime scenes and took my own photos, but it was at the funeral home, and I hadn't gone by to get it. I'd have to make do with the pictures Officer Riley was taking.

"Let's do it," I said, nodding as Detective Cole walked up.

I liked working with Cole. He was a good guy and a good cop. He was all legs and moved with a slow, lanky gait. His cowboy boots were caked with mud and grass, and his Wranglers fit well enough that he was never without female attention. He wore a black down vest over his denim shirt, and it mostly covered his holster and the badge on his belt.

"Doc," he said in greeting. "Long time no see."

"Yeah," I agreed. "I was starting to think crime was a thing of the past."

Cole smiled. "We had a lucky stretch. Now we just gotta hope we won't be playing catch-up for the next three months."

"Lovely thought," I said.

"This thing is going to be harder to get out than it was to get in," Cole said, nodding at the cops trying to lift the pipe out of the ground. "Once you push the pipe into that hole, gravity pretty much takes care of the rest."

"Our thoughts too," Jack said.

Martinez and Riley had the unfortunate task of lifting the pipe, and they were both straining to get it out of the ground.

"When it falls back, it's going to fall hard," I said. "It could compromise the body."

Jack nodded and clapped Cole on the shoulder. "Let's get dirty," he said and went to position himself behind the body. Riley and Martinez managed to lift it little by little, until the body started to tilt backward.

"Got it," Jack said. "Let's bring him down slow."

By the time the body was on the ground, Martinez and Riley were sweating and panting for breath, and Jack and Cole had stains on the front of their shirts and jeans that I didn't want to think about.

I reached into my bag for a pair of gloves and slipped them on quickly. The straw hat had fallen off the victim when he'd been laid down, and I winced at the sight of the battered and swollen face. An eye was missing, but I wasn't sure if it had been done deliberately or by a vulture. They tended to go for soft tissue first, and the area around the socket was jagged and torn.

Announcing their displeasure, the vultures hissed and made a low grunting sound overhead, and something soft and wet plopped onto my shoulder. I sighed and picked up the piece of intestine.

"Gross," I said.

An industrial-strength wire had been used around his neck to tie him to the pole, and the same wires had been used around each wrist. The edges were sharp where the wire had been cut.

"Check this out," I said to Jack, lifting the victim's shirt sleeve so he could see the silver wire.

"Looks like high-gauge fence wire," he said. "Any farm in the state would have it lying around. Don't try to twist it off with your fingers. You're going to need pliers."

"I've got some in the trunk of my unit," Cole said, heading off to his truck. He was back quickly and untwisted the metal at each wrist. It was time consuming.

"The killer drives out here in the middle of nowhere with a body in the trunk," I said, thinking it through out loud. "It's pitch black, and this guy probably weighs two hundred pounds. If the victim was dragged from a car to here his whole backside would be covered in mud, and it's not."

"So someone carried him," Cole said. "Or maybe they put him on a piece of cardboard and dragged him over. There are tire tracks all over hell and back, so we didn't pick up on any drag marks."

I nodded, trying to work through it in my mind. "How far is it between here and Cotton's house?" I asked.

"A couple of hundred yards," Jack said. "Maybe a little more."

"Once the killer got here, in the dark, and carried the body to where we're standing, then he had to go about the process of wiring him up. Look how long it's taken Cole to untwist the wire. He couldn't do it in the dark. He'd need a high-powered flashlight."

"I doubt a flashlight could be seen from the house unless Cotton was looking straight at it," Cole said.

"Killer had brass balls," Martinez said, his hand resting on his weapon out of habit.

"We've got wire at the neck, both wrists, and ankles," Cole said, dropping each length of wire into an evidence bag as he untied them."

I could see the areas in question clearer now that the wire was gone. "He's got ligature marks. The bruising indicates it occurred antemortem, and it's a different material than the wire. I might be able to get some fibers once I get him back to the lab. It looks like rope burn."

"There's got to be another wire I'm missing," Cole said, patting the victim's legs and arms down gently.

"Look," I said, pulling the waistband of his trousers down carefully so as not to disturb what remained of his abdomen. "A man like this would wear a belt with his expensive suit, wouldn't he?"

"Yeah," Jack said, crouching down beside me. "We didn't find one as we canvased the area, but we'll keep looking. The killer might have kept a souvenir."

I unclasped the trousers so I could pull them down a little farther, exposing the metal wire around his waist. Fortunately, it was twisted in front of him instead of behind him. The sharp ends had penetrated the dermis and I pressed down on the skin to release the wire so Cole could unwind it.

"This wasn't a fast job," Jack said. "The killer knew the area, knew how much time he had, and what equipment he'd need. Once he had him secured to the pole, then he had to get him upright. Once he was upright, the killer lifted the victim's shirt, gutted him, and then tucked his shirt back into his pants. We haven't found any evidence other than what the vultures scattered around. The killer cleaned up well."

"That's messed up," Martinez said.

"It takes all kinds," Jack said. "Our job is to put whoever did this away. Let's make sure we follow all protocol on this. Pick up every scrap of paper, cigarette butt, or pocket lint, even if it seems unimportant. Let's get a team out by the entrance to this road and see if we can pull any tire tracks. Maybe we'll get lucky."

We heard gravel crunching beneath tires and all turned to look as another black Suburban pulled in directly behind mine.

Martinez whistled low and long. "Well, this day just got a whole lot better," he said, running a hand through his dark hair to make sure it was perfect.

Martinez had a nickname around the squad room as the GQ cop. He was always put together, his clothes pressed and probably nicer than his salary could afford, and his hair was always styled. He was a lady's man, though to be fair, I had yet to meet a cop who didn't consider himself a lady's man. You could hang a uniform on a light post and the badge bunnies would throw themselves at it.

"Leave my intern alone," I said, rolling my eyes. "She has no idea how to handle a wolf like you."

"I'm hurt," Martinez said, grabbing his chest. "How dare you think I'd treat my future wife that way."

Cole snorted out a laugh. "In your dreams, Martinez. She's so far out of your league you'd be lucky to clean the dugout."

"I'm always up for a challenge. I've been known to play in the Ivy Leagues a time or two myself. I've never had any complaints."

The cops closest to us snickered under their breaths, and then the insults started flying. I looked over at Jack and saw the corner of his mouth tilted and the sparkle of laughter in his eyes.

Fortunately, Lily could handle herself. I could only assume that when you looked like she did, it was important to learn how to ward off unwanted advances. Lily was stunning. She had the sculpted features of a supermodel and a body that belonged to a Kardashian. Jack had to tell several of the officers to tone down the excited looks at crime scenes when she arrived. It didn't make a good impression to the community to see cops grinning like loons over a dead body.

She'd been my intern for the past eight months or so, and she was quite simply, amazing. Her brains and her sarcastic wit far surpassed her beauty, and I liked her immensely. She was going to graduate in December, and then it'd be just me and my assistant, Sheldon Durkus, unless the university approved my request for another intern for the spring semester. I'd found it was good to have a buffer between myself and Sheldon so I didn't kill him.

Sheldon was the complete opposite of Lily. He reminded me of a mole, coming into the light for the first time as he got out of the passenger side of the Suburban. He was a small doughy man with Coke bottle glasses and a comb-over. He was in his early twenties, and he made socially awkward people seem totally normal. Sheldon was my assistant at the funeral home, and he was finishing up getting his mortician's license. He wasn't great with people, and he had a tendency to say the wrong thing to grieving families at the wrong time, but his embalming technique and organizational skills were top notch, so I tried to keep him contained from clients unless I absolutely couldn't help it.

Our relationship had changed over the last couple of months. Sheldon had been with me at the mortician's convention when a serial killer had wreaked havoc at our hotel—the death hotel, as Chuck Grable had called it. Sheldon had been a little harder to deal with since the traumatic event. He was dealing with guilt over the fact that he'd had a romantic relationship with thc killer, and she'd been using him for her own gains. So Sheldon's attitude had gone from naïve schoolboy who quoted useless facts at inappropriate times to a belligerent preteen who quoted useless facts all the time.

Part of me felt motherly toward Sheldon, even though he still lived with his own mother, but another part of me had needed some distance from him once we'd returned to Bloody Mary. I'd managed not to strangle him since he'd come back to work, which was a win in my book, but I was thinking he probably needed to see a therapist.

Lily and Sheldon carried the gurney toward us, two opposites of the same coin. I'd learned the dead spoke to different people in different ways, and Lily and Sheldon were perfect examples of that. They both understood the dead in their own ways, and more importantly, they respected the dead.

"Well," Lily said, looking down at the victim. "That's different."

My lips twitched, but I refrained from smiling. Gallows humor was something we were all familiar with. Outsiders might never understand it, but it was necessary for our mental survival.

"Let's get him back to the lab before these vultures lose their patience."

"Speaking of vultures," Lily said, "We passed Floyd Parker on the way here. I wouldn't be surprised if he wasn't far behind."

I grunted and moved out of the way so they could get the gurney next to the body. I hated Floyd Parker. He was a viper. And it only made things worse that we'd had a romantic entanglement during my med school years. It was a regret I'd take with me to the grave.

My last encounter with Floyd had ended with him getting a fist to the nose. He'd been impeding an investigation and pushed his way in a little too close to the victim. Coroners had more authority than most people realized, and he'd been lucky I hadn't had him arrested. I wasn't sure why Floyd had fallen off my radar the last few months, but it had been nice not to run into him every time I turned a corner. I was guessing that luck was about to change.

"I don't think Floyd is going to be of concern," Jack said easily.

I narrowed my eyes, wondering what I'd missed. Maybe it hadn't been luck that had kept Floyd out of my path.

"On three," I said as we gathered around the body.

We lifted the victim and put him carefully into a body bag, and then lifted him onto the gurney. He was a big man, probably two hundred pounds, though part of that weight could have been because of the swelling of organs and tissues.

"I'll meet you guys back at the funeral home," I said to Lily and Sheldon.

"What about the donuts?" Sheldon asked, accusingly. "Emmy Lu said you were bringing donuts this morning, but you never came." Sweat beaded on his upper lip from the effort it took to carry the body to the Suburban and load him into the back.

"Yeah, sorry about that," I said sarcastically. "This pesky murder took priority."

"I didn't eat my oatmeal because I was expecting donuts," he said, my sarcasm going right over his head. "If I don't eat regularly I get light-headed."

"Come on, sport," Lily said, patting him on the shoulder. "The sooner we get the body back, the sooner you can get your donut."

"Did you know over ten billion donuts are consumed in this country every year?" Sheldon asked.

"Then I'm glad we're doing our part to help the numbers," I said.

"Wait a sec," Martinez said. "You've got donuts? Have you had them in your Suburban the whole time?"

"I thought I smelled Lady Jane's," Cole said. "But figured it was wishful thinking."

"You take another step toward my donuts, Martinez, and you die," I said. "And you did not smell donuts from inside my vehicle. Especially not over the stench of rotting intestines."

"I'm a cop," Cole said. "I can sniff out a donut better than a K9 sniffing out drugs."

"That must be a real attention getter on your resume," I said, making the others chuckle.

"I want to ask the homeowner a couple more questions," Jack said.

"I'll come with you," I told him. "They'll need time to unload the body." I looked at Martinez and hit the remote for the Suburban so the doors locked. "Stay away from my donuts."

"Harsh," Martinez said.

I walked with Jack across the road and the long expanse of yard to the white farmhouse. There were chickens running loose, and a pen of goats bleated at the disturbance as we walked by. I was sweating by the time we made it to the house, and I wished I'd left my bag in the car instead of hauling it with me.

"Hey, Sheriff," a man called out, and Jack and I turned.

A man in worn denim and a white T-shirt was walking toward us from the barn, waving his hand.

Jack waved back, and we changed our direction to meet the man halfway. "I take it that's Cotton?" I asked.

"You got it," Jack said, and then he reached out to shake the man's hand as we drew near.

"Sorry about that," Cotton said. "I had things to tend to in the barn." Then he turned to me and nodded his head, "Ma'am."

"This is Dr. Graves," Jack said. "Jaye, this is Donald Cotton. He found the victim this morning."

"That had to be an experience," I said.

"I've had better mornings," he agreed, his mouth in a grim line.

Donald Cotton was a good-sized man a few inches taller than my own five foot eight. He was somewhere in his late forties, maybe early fifties, and the breadth of his shoulders and the muscles in his biceps described a man who labored hard from day to day. His shirt was grimy with the morning's work, and the leather work gloves he held in his hand looked like they'd seen better days.

"I think he might be past the point of needing a doctor," Cotton told me.

I smiled. "I'm not that kind of doctor. I'm the coroner."

"Ahh, I guess that makes more sense. I don't know who could do a thing like this. Why someone would pick my land to do it on. I've never had a bit of trouble. Not even kids sneaking out here to get high or mess around."

"We're going to need a list of all your farmhands," Jack said. "It makes sense it'd be someone familiar with your property."

"Yeah," Cotton said. "But I'd like to think I know the men I work side by side with every day. I can't imagine any of them doing something like this. But I'll get you a list. It's not that long. And most of my workers are transient. I or one of the other guys will head down to the hardware store and pick up a few day laborers here and there."

"Just whoever you can think of will be a good place to start," Jack said. "When did you notice the body?"

"I got up about four thirty like usual," he said, "And then I'm out at the barn by five. It's still dark out then, but I could hear the buzzards so I knew something had died out in the field. It happens from time to time, so I went about getting the cows started milking. The field hands start showing up about seven now that it's getting light a little later, and I could hear them driving up. But when I came out of the barn I could see the buzzards still circling, and I knew it wasn't just a small animal. They can pluck a chicken clean in half an hour. So I got my flashlight thinking a wolf might have gotten into the sheep pen."

He swallowed hard and looked away. "But it wasn't no sheep. He was up there plain as day, and I shooed the buzzards away best I could and called 911."

"You didn't notice anything last night?" Jack asked.

Cotton shook his head. "Can't say I did. I did my last check in the barn around eight o'clock and then I headed in for the night. I'm an early riser so I tuck in early. There wasn't anything out there, and I would've seen trucks coming or going."

"Do you live here alone?" I asked. "Could anyone else have heard something?"

"It's just me," he said, his mouth thinning again. "My wife died seven years ago. Cancer."

"I'm sorry to hear that," Jack said.

"I've thought about selling the farm and moving," he said. "But it's all I know. It keeps me busy when my mind starts to think about her. I hope y'all find who did this."

"If you feel you're in danger I can have a deputy ride out and check on you," Jack said.

"I'll be fine," Cotton said. "I've got my own protection, and I'm not afraid to use it."

3

Bloody Mary was an acquired taste. There were those who'd move in from D.C. or other cities and commute to work, thinking they wanted a cheap place to live with good schools and a simpler way of life. But most of those people didn't last long.

Bloody Mary was mostly multigenerational families who talked about things that happened a hundred years ago as if it were yesterday. The life was definitely simpler, but most found it to be too simple. Grocery stores, gas stations, and movie theaters weren't easy to come by. People didn't have their faces stuck in cell phone screens all day, and they didn't pay all that much attention to what was happening in the rest of the world.

For the 2,900 residents of this sleepy town—give or take a few—life was about achieving the American Dream—working hard, watching your children grow, and hot coffee served with a freshly baked slice of gossip. The houses were small, the yards neat, and businesses were about customer service.

The funeral home was just a block from the town square on the corner of Catherine of Aragon and Anne Boleyn. It was a three-story, red-bricked Colonial with white columns in front. It had been built at the turn of the twentieth century, and had originally belonged to my great-grandparents when they'd decided to get into the undertaking business. It was such a specialized skill back then that people came from all over the state if they could afford to pay for an embalming and burial. Needless to say, my ancestors made out like bandits. The funeral home was all I had left to show for a legacy, but all in all, it wasn't a bad one.

I'd gotten lucky during the storm. A large branch had split from one of the two massive oak trees that stood like sentries on the front lawn and fallen inches from the roof. Someone was supposed to come out and remove it at some point, but Bloody Mary time didn't work the same as time in other places. The fallen limb might be removed today or sometime a month from now.

I pulled into the carport behind Lily and Sheldon, grabbed my bag and the donuts, and headed inside. I hadn't bothered to change out of my coveralls or boots since they were covered in mud. Jack parked his unit street side and got out, eyeing the giant limb on his way over.

"I'll give Lenny Green a call and see if he can move you up on the priority list," he said, taking my things so I could get out of the car without falling on my face.

"The good news is no one has died this week, so I don't have any viewings scheduled," I told him.

"You might want to hold off making that declaration. We've got a body count after the tornadoes."

I grimaced. "Anyone local?"

"No, most of the victims came from Newcastle. They got hit the hardest."

"I don't mean to sound like a nagging wife..." He grinned when I said this. "But you don't look so good. When was the last time you ate? Or slept?"

"Good question," he said. "But I'm not sure either of those things is on the schedule as of now."

I clamped my lips shut and decided I needed to take matters into my own hands. God wouldn't have given women the ability to manipulate if he hadn't wanted them to use it on stubborn men.

"Come on, then," I said, and headed up the ramp attached to the carport. I left my muddy boots at the door.

Lily and Sheldon had already rolled the body through the mudroom and into the big kitchen. My lab was just off the kitchen, and Sheldon typed in the code to unlock the thick metal door. There was a whooshing sound as the door unsealed, and Lily held it open while Sheldon pushed the body into the elevator. The temperature was decidedly colder down there, and I saw Lily shiver as she followed behind Sheldon.

"Just roll him into station one and leave him in the bag," I told them. "I'll be down in a minute. I need to change."

I put the donuts and my medical bag on the island and went to start a pot of coffee. Jack was asleep on his feet. He dropped onto one of the barstools, and didn't say anything as I got eggs out of the fridge and the bread from the pantry. I didn't know if he was in shock from the sight of me cooking or if he was sleeping with his eyes open.

Emmy Lu kept the kitchen stocked with necessities, for staff as well as for me if I had to work late. I was grateful to have her, because I never thought of things like stocking the kitchen or putting extra toilet paper in the bathrooms. If there wasn't a body attached to it, I wasn't great with the details.

I probably added too much salt to the eggs and butter to the pan, but by the time I was finished, it mostly looked like French toast. I put the plate in front of Jack, poured him a cup of coffee, and kissed him on top of the head. Jack was the extrovert of the two of us, and I wasn't sure I'd ever heard him be this quiet for as long as he had.

I left him in peace and went to my office, so I could strip out of the coveralls and find another pair of shoes that wasn't caked with mud. All I had in the closet were a pair of dress shoes I kept for viewings and a pair of white sneakers. I picked the white sneakers. The victim wasn't going to be impressed by my shoe choice. I washed my hands thoroughly, and splashed some cold water on my face before getting my lab coat off the hook on the back of the door.

I was buttoning it up when I walked back into the kitchen. The donuts were gone, but Jack was standing at the sink, rinsing off the plate.

"Thanks for that," he said, not turning around. "You did good. Now that I know you can cook, you might have to do it more often."

"French toast and mac 'n' cheese are pretty much where my talents end." I paused for a second, not sure what to say. This breakneck pace when disaster struck was nothing new. Jack thrived on it. We'd been in tougher and more stressful situations, so seeing him this exhausted was worrisome. "You okay?" I asked.

"Better now," he said. "Just getting old and tired."

"You're not that old," I said.

"It feels like it," he said, finally turning to face me. "Sometimes I wonder if the job is worth it, that's all."

My brows rose in surprise. Jack had lived and breathed the job since he'd first set foot in the academy. He'd been born to be a cop. He was brilliant at it, and he was a good leader. Even when he'd taken three bullets to the chest and watched his friends die, he'd never wondered if the job had been worth it.

"You make a difference, Jack," I said. "Don't ever doubt that."

He sighed and scrubbed a hand over his stubble. "I think the politics are just getting to me. I love the job. I always have. But I hate the bureaucratic bullshit. I hate the meetings and the paperwork and being diplomatic. Sometimes I miss handling a situation with a cannon instead of a scalpel." He smiled as he said that, and I realized I'd been holding my breath. I let it out slowly.

"The election is next month," he said. "And I'm not even sure I care if I win or not."

"You're going to win by a landslide," I told him. "No one in their right mind would vote for Harley Grubbs. He's a hundred years old, and he has so much hair in his ears he can't hear."

"Floyd Parker is going to be on the ballot," he said. "He turned his paperwork in at the last minute."

I saw red for several seconds before the haze started to clear. "That son of a—"

Jack held up his hands and said, "He's had a bone to pick ever since you gave him that bloody nose.

Actually, he's had a bone to pick with you since you ended things between you. He figures if he can beat me then he can get rid of you too."

"He's a moron, and I hate his guts," I said. "And you'd better campaign for all you're worth, Jack Lawson, because there's not a snowball's chance in hell that a no-good turnip like Floyd Parker could ever beat you without cheating. So don't put it past him to try something like that. No wonder he's been so quiet lately. We're going to crush him," I said, pounding my fist in my hand.

Jack grinned and I saw the tension go out of his shoulders. It wasn't just about Floyd Parker. Jack was a cop to his bones. And if he left the job, I worried how not being a cop would affect him. It was a slippery slope to leave the only identity you'd ever known and try to figure out who you were without a gun and badge. There was a reason the suicide rate was even higher for those who retired from the job.

"Listen," I said, choosing my words carefully. "You know I'm behind you a hundred percent, right? If you decided you wanted to quit the job today and spend the rest of your life in a hammock on the beach, I'm right there with you. We're a team, no matter what."

"I know that," he said, closing the distance between us so he was only a breath away. His hand came up and touched the side of my cheek.

"But I'd be remiss in not saying that you were made for this job. The people here need you. Do you want to leave them in the hands of someone like Floyd Parker? If it's the politics that bothers you maybe you can change things up some. Give some promotions. Let some of the other guys deal with the crap that sucks the life out of you. Do the things that made you fall in love with this job to begin with."

"That's a lot of wisdom, wife," he said, leaning down to kiss me softly. "And very good advice. Maybe if I hadn't been so knotted up with all this I could have come to the same conclusion. But I'm glad you did. Thank you."

"Hey, that's what I'm here for," I said. "Advice, sex, and French toast. You're a well-kept man."

He snorted out a laugh and put his arm around my shoulder, leading me toward the door to the lab.

"Come on," he said. "Get me my fingerprints. We can worry about kicking Floyd Parker's ass later."

I punched in the code for the door and waited for the mechanisms to unlock before allowing us entry. The lab was in the basement of the funeral home, and it was an addition my parents had added about twenty years ago. I'd grown up thinking that all embalming areas had this kind of security until I went to medical school and saw that even the best morgues in the state weren't protected like Fort Knox.

My parents' setup had more to do with their smuggling operation than the protection of the deceased inside. Whatever the reason, I'd lucked out by inheriting one of the top unknown facilities in the state. My security was the best, and my equipment was top of the line. And the guilt I'd felt in the past over benefitting from my parents' crimes was long gone.

I liked taking the stairs instead of the lift, so we headed into the depths of the cool basement. Lights came on, blindingly white, the second our feet touched the stairs. Lily and Sheldon had left the victim on the gurney in the body bag like I'd requested. I saw Jack take a deep breath and hold it in before slowly releasing it, and I hid my smile. He could stare at dead bodies all day, but the lingering smell of embalming fluid made him queasy every time. He rarely came into the lab with me.

I grabbed a pair of gloves and my camera and then unzipped the body bag. I took my own set of pictures, and then I went ahead and cut off his clothes. I'd learned the hard way to do this while the victim was still in the bag so any fibers or evidence would be caught in the bag. I had a machine to hang the clothes in that would shake off any particulates for me to put into evidence later.

"Hey, Alexa," I said to the black cylinder in the corner. "Play autopsy playlist."

"You have an autopsy playlist?" Jack asked, clearly amused.

"Of course," I said, carefully removing the bags from the victim's hands. Bon Jovi's "Wanted, Dead or Alive" came over the speakers and I heard Jack chuckle.

I took samples from beneath the victim's nails and labeled them, and then took a blood sample to send off to the lab in Richmond, and I took another blood sample so I could run my own tests. I had a lot of the equipment the Richmond lab had, but it was always good to have a backup report, especially in a homicide.

Technology had made examinations a lot more convenient over the past decade or so. I was able to take fingerprints digitally, like they do at the DMV, as long as the prints hadn't been damaged by weather or water.

"It's a clear set," I told Jack, sending him an email copy of the prints as well as printing them on card stock so he could take them with him. Not everyone in the county was as keen on modern technology as we were.

I took a step back from the body, trying to decide how to proceed. Normally, I'd put straps around him and use the lift to carry someone his size to my autopsy table, but I wasn't entirely sure that was the best way to keep all his guts in place.

"Let's just lift him," Jack said, going over to the table to put a pair of gloves on. "I'd rather not have to pick up intestines off the floor."

"Spoilsport," I said, rolling the gurney as close to the autopsy table as I could. "On three. One—two—" and then we lifted him to the metal table.

"And that's my call to head out," Jack said, leaning over to kiss me goodbye. He stripped off his gloves and tossed them in the trash. "Give me a call when you've finished the autopsy. Maybe we'll have an ID by then."

"10-4, Sheriff Hot Stuff," I said. His look was not amused. "What?" I asked. "This book I read said to remember to compliment and pursue your spouse every day so you don't fall into a rut. I'll loan you my copy if you want to read it."

"Sounds like a real page-turner," he said. "So what should I call you? Dr. Fine Ass? Maybe something paying homage to that heart-shaped freckle on your breast. You know that drives me crazy. Dr. Love Freckle?"

"No," I said, shaking my head. "Definitely not Dr. Love Freckle."

"Just as well," Jack said. "I think that was the name of a porno one of the guys was talking about at the station."

I snickered and went to collect the clothes that had been left in the body bag. "I'll concede to Dr. Fine Ass. Or just DFA for short. It's like my rapper name. The Notorious DFA."

"This conversation escalated quickly," he said. "I think the smell has gone to your brain. Text me later, Notorious DFA."

My attention was already back on the victim by the time I heard the door closing behind him. I turned on the spotlight, and got to work. I generally made notations with a recorder instead of stopping what I was doing to write notes every few seconds, so I turned off the music and turned on my recorder.

"October twenty-eighth. Eleven forty-three a.m.," I said. "Homicide. Victim is Caucasian male, brown hair, brown eyes. Age approximated between fifty-five and sixty-five years of age. No tattoos or birthmarks. Slight scarring behind ears indicate possible plastic surgery procedure. No other visible surgical marks.

"Cause of death could not be determined from crime scene. Time of death is at least twenty-four hours, but most likely somewhere between thirty-six and forty-eight hours based on stages of decomp and insect activity at crime scene."

I adjusted the light and took photographs of the ligature marks around his ankles and wrists. "Victim was restrained. Fibers found embedded in the skin are being collected to admit into evidence. It looks like natural rope fibers."

I studied every inch of the victim's exterior. "Kneecaps have been broken. And there looks to be burn marks on the thighs and around the groin.

Maybe from a cattle prod or taser?" I skipped over his midsection for now, knowing the wound there had been postmortem. "Fingers on both hands are broken. And there are more burn marks under the armpit area on the right side. External examination also reveals multiple broken ribs." But no cause of death, I thought to myself.

I moved my light again, this time to the face, and examined the wound around the missing eye. "Right eye is missing. Wounds are jagged in nature, making it possible for the loss to be due to a scavenger." I pulled down the magnifier so I could take a closer look. There was a section of skin around the inner eye that looked as if it had been sliced with something sharp. I made the notations, and then checked the skull for any damage.

"Hematoma at the base of the skull. Feels similar to injuries consistent with the butt end of a pistol. Most probably from impact of the initial incapacitation."

I went back to the wound across his abdomen. "Victim was gutted postmortem." I took out my ruler and measured the depth of the wound. "Cut is almost two inches deep, and it's a clean slice of fourteen inches. There are no hesitations in the cut, and indications suggest most likely done with a sharp smooth blade with no serrations."

I turned off the recorder and put a block beneath his back to arch the chest up, and then I went about the task of cleaning the body. It was all routine. I took x-rays and developed them, placing the images on the light wall above my desk. It showed me what I already knew—that the victim was beaten and tortured. I noted a couple of old breaks on his right ulna and left femur. Most likely childhood breaks from the remodeling.

But what would tell me the real story was on the inside. I turned my recorder back on, grabbed my scalpel, and made the first Y-cut. I had just removed the ribs when my cell phone started to ring. Jack didn't normally call when he knew I was in the middle of an autopsy, so I figured it must be important. I took off my gloves and answered the phone.

"What's up?" I asked.

"We've already got a hit on the fingerprints," he said. "He was in the system."

"Criminal or public servant?" I asked, thinking those were the two most likely categories of people to have their prints on file.

"A little of both," he said. "John Donnelly."

"Why does that name sound familiar?" I asked.

"Because he's the slimeball attorney that just got Terrence Newman released from prison on a technicality."

"Ohhhh," I said, looking at the victim on my table in a new light. "That's why he sounds familiar. I guess someone wasn't too happy with Mr. Donnelly. He's been worked over pretty good."

"The list is going to be a mile long," Jack said.

"You'd think someone this high profile would have been reported missing," I said.

"I'm not sure John Donnelly is the kind of person anyone would miss. I'm going to get some more data on him, and I'm keeping this from public record until we can find out if he had any family."

Jack didn't bother to disguise his dislike for the victim. "Well," I said. "This sucks."

"Yeah, it does. People like John Donnelly don't deserve justice. And I don't say that lightly. In fact, I'm not sure I've ever said it about a victim before. But the world is better off without him. Sometimes death is too good for people."

"Maybe so," I said, trying to think of the right words to say. Jack lived by a very solid code of honor. He believed in justice. And he believed our job was to serve the victim. What he'd just said sounded like something that would come out of my mouth. We hadn't always seen eye to eye on the cases we'd worked. I had a tendency to work in the gray areas a little. But not Jack.

"Maybe he did deserve to die," I said. "That's not our call to make. That's between him and God. But that doesn't mean there's not a killer out there. Maybe he felt killing John Donnelly was justifiable. But maybe he's got a taste for it now, and has decided his own brand of justice is more satisfying.

If we can't find the killer for this victim, we need to find the killer for future victims."

Jack sighed. "I know you're right. I was just venting. Chalk it up to lack of sleep. Meet me at the station when you're done with the autopsy, and we'll start asking questions. I want to know why no one bothered to report him missing."

Jack hung up, and I was left alone with John Donnelly. I put on a fresh pair of gloves and got back to work.

I stared down into the gaping wound where his eye had once been. "You should know by now that in our line of work, justice is always served," I told him. "Looks like you got yours."

4

Two hours later, I had cause of death in hand. I didn't send any digital files, considering the news would leak faster than a rusty bucket if I had. No one could keep their mouths shut in this town. So I printed everything out and sealed it in an envelope.

There wasn't much more I could do with Mr. Donnelly at this point, so I rolled him into the cooler and cleaned up. By the time I got into the Suburban to head to the sheriff's office, my stomach was growling. My early morning donuts didn't have much staying power. I thought about Jack too, knew the French toast was probably the last thing he'd put in his mouth other than coffee, so I swung through a drive-thru and picked up a couple of hamburgers.

It felt like death clung to me, so I rolled down my windows, enjoying the cool afternoon and bright sunshine. It wouldn't be long before these occasional warm days turned into snow and freezing temperatures.

Everyone else must've had the same thought, because the town square was bustling with people and cars. Businesses had their doors open and goods were displayed on the sidewalk. Banners hung across the streets advertising the Halloween party on the square. The courthouse looked like it belonged at a Halloween party year-round, and it loomed tall and Gothic in the center of the square, the gargoyle faces on the corners smiling down obscenely.

The jail, sheriff's office, fire station and civil building were on the opposite side, attached together in a space that was desperate for expansion, but had nowhere to grow but up. The good news was that a bond had passed to build a new fire station, so once they vacated the premises, Jack would be able to do the renovations to the sheriff's office and jail that were necessary for the county.

I parked in one of the employee spots in front of the jail, and if I'd been paying attention to who was in front of me, I would've parked three blocks away and walked. Tom Daly stood on the sidewalk, staring straight at me. I knew I had a deer-in-the-headlights look, and I wondered if I just stayed as still as possible if I'd become invisible. I debated on whether or not to get out of the car, but then he looked at me oddly and waved.

I blew out a sigh and got out of the car. "Hey, Tom," I said awkwardly. "How's it going?"

"It's going," he said, shrugging. "How are things with you? Congratulations on your marriage. I guess I haven't seen you in a while."

Guilt swamped me. He really was a nice guy. "Thanks," I said. "Things have been busy. I'll stop in the shop one day this week and catch you up. We caught a homicide this morning, so I'm heading in to see Jack."

"I'll look forward to seeing you," he said, his hangdog expression brightening a little. "Tell Jack hello for me, and that he's got our support for reelection."

"Will do," I said, my chest tight. "See you soon."

I walked past him and up the steps that led to the sheriff's office. I waved my way past the sergeant manning the front desk, and headed back to Jack's office. He was just hanging up the phone when I walked in.

"Good timing," he said, eyeing the fast-food bag in my hand. "Is that for me?"

"Yep," I said, putting the bag and the envelope with the autopsy findings on his desk.

"I love you desperately," he said. "Have I told you that today?"

"It's always worth repeating," I said. "I just ran into Tom Daly. We'll be stopping by sometime this week to buy donuts for the station."

Jack's lips twitched. "You're trying to make my officers fat. But in this case, I'm all for it."

"Why did you say I had good timing?" I asked, handing Jack a burger and keeping the other for myself. I sat down in the seat across from him.

"Because I just got off the phone with an officer in Richmond who says they found an abandoned red Porsche Cayenne in a supermarket parking lot. The manager called the police and they came out and ran the plates. Guess who it belongs to?"

"I'm going to go with John Donnelly. There aren't that many people in King George who could afford to drive around in a car like that."

"Bingo," he said. "The officer was calling so I could do a welfare check."

"I can tell you on good authority that's pointless. He's very dead and in my cooler."

"Did you find cause of death?"

"More or less," I said. "Let's just say that Donnelly did not treat his body well. My overall ruling is cardiac arrest. He was tortured, but not to the extent we've seen from other victims. His heart literally exploded from the trauma. My guess is he had a heart attack and died before the killer was able to enjoy his job too much."

"Yikes," Jack said.

"But here's the kicker," I continued. "It's a miracle he didn't drop dead of a heart attack before the killer got hold of him. He was in terrible shape. He had blockages in all of his arteries, his liver was a mess and showed signs of chronic alcoholism. He would've needed a transplant in the next year. And he had lung cancer to top it all off."

"Geez," Jack said. "Ticking time bomb. You'd never guess any of that by seeing him in court. Everyone knows he has a drinking problem, but by outward appearances, he seemed to be in good shape."

"He's had plastic surgery," I said. "Face-lift, liposuction, calf implants, neck lift, eye lift, and nose job. And it looks like he's been getting regular Botox injections."

"He'd have a doctor for the injections, right?" Jack asked, and I nodded. "We'll need to find out who it was and talk to them. No one wants to hire an attorney at that price who looks like they're about to keel over. Appearances mean something."

"Maybe he should've paid as much attention to his insides," I said. "Between the cancer, his heart, and his liver, he probably had a matter of weeks, maybe months, to live."

Jack grunted. "Anything else of interest?"

"Yeah, I ran a tox screen, and his blood alcohol level was .16. Only other contents in his stomach was snack mix—peanuts, pretzels, beer nuts."

"Like you find at a bar," he said.

"My thoughts too," I agreed. "He was twice the legal limit, but leaving a bar and driving home drunk would've been par for the course for a guy like Donnelly."

"I haven't released his name yet," Jack said. "I was waiting on you to notify next of kin. He's got a few kids scattered across the tristate area and a couple of ex-wives. When I was digging, I also found a woman he got pregnant about ten years ago, but he paid her a couple of million dollars to move to another state and have the kid on her own. His current live-in is a woman named Kimberly Kloss. Her name is on the lease of a townhouse they have in Manhattan, and her name also comes up on the title on another red Porsche, only hers is a 911. I'm very interested to ask why she never reported him missing."

"It just so happens my schedule is free for the rest of the evening," I said. "Why don't we pay Ms. Kloss a visit?

John Donnelly's home was in the High Pointe neighborhood in King George Proper. It was a gated community on the golf course, and everyone drove their golf carts around to luncheons and parties at the club. I much preferred our privacy out in the country and our view of the Potomac.

Jack showed his badge to the gate guard and we motored through a winding neighborhood with beautiful homes and perfectly manicured lawns. There was a large pond with a fountain spurting water in several different arcs, and there were groups scattered along the golf course finishing their afternoon tee times.

Donnelly's house was a stucco monstrosity with a Spanish tile roof and a lot of windows. I was more interested in the two black cars parked in the front drive with their trunks popped open.

"Looks like someone is taking a trip," I said, noting the brand-name luggage piled into each trunk.

"Someone is about to be disappointed," Jack said, parking his Tahoe behind the second car.

We got out of the car and crossed the pavers to oversized double doors that stood wide open. There were people everywhere, and they all seemed to be in a hurry. Women carried stacks of towels and clothing, and men hauled suitcases. A woman was on a ladder, dusting the giant chandelier in the foyer, and another woman was putting new flowers in the big urn on the table.

"Excuse me," Jack said, stepping just over the threshold. "Is there a Kimberly Kloss here?"

Everyone ignored Jack and kept working as if their lives depended on it.

"Kimberly Kloss," Jack said, a little louder this time.

"José," a woman yelled from upstairs. "See who that is and tell them to go away, and get these people moving. We're going to be late!" She had the voice of a bull horn.

A man in black slacks and a short-sleeved white button-down came from one of the back rooms looking frazzled, and he shot a look of such malice in the direction of the voice upstairs that I involuntarily took a step toward the stairs in case he decided he was going to toss her off the balcony.

"I'm sorry," he said, his accent thick. He tried to shoo us back outside, and I raised a brow. "Ms. Kloss and Mr. Donnelly are leaving for vacation."

"Well, he's half right," I said, looking at Jack.

"They are late to the airport," José insisted. "They do not have time to buy whatever you are selling."

Jack showed the man his badge, and José immediately stopped in his tracks and his gaze went toward the small woman cleaning the chandelier.

"We have no problems here," José said. "Everyone has papers."

"I'm not here for that," Jack said. "We need to speak with Ms. Kloss. And you should probably let her know she's going to miss her flight."

"Mr. Donnelly?" José asked, his brow furrowed. "It's Mr. Donnelly, isn't it? I knew something was not right when he did not come home. But sometimes he would stay out for a day or two, just to have some peace and quiet." He pointed to the ceiling. "You heard her so you can understand why."

My mouth twitched, but I managed to avoid a smile.

"He would usually tell me when he was going to be gone," he continued. "But sometimes he didn't."

"And you are?" Jack asked.

"José Sosa. I'm the house manager."

"We found Mr. Donnelly's body early this morning," Jack said. "We really need to talk to Ms. Kloss."

José's lips tightened and he nodded. "Come with me. It will save time." We followed José up the rounded staircase to the second level.

"How long have you worked for Mr. Donnelly?" I asked.

"Twelve years," José said.

"And he would do this often? Just not come home for a couple of days?"

"Mr. Donnelly enjoyed celebrating his wins in court. And he won a lot. He would usually let me know his plans for the day, but sometimes he would change them last minute. I kept a calendar of his social events and travel plans, but he was a grown man who could come and go as he pleased."

"Were his changes in plans ever due to his drinking?" I asked.

"Mr. Donnelly enjoyed celebrating his wins in court. And he won a lot."

"Do you mean his drinking?" I asked.

José's lips tightened again. "It's not for me to say. My job is to manage the household and make sure everything runs smoothly, whether Mr. Donnelly is here or not."

"What about Ms. Kloss?" Jack asked. "How long has she been living here?"

José's eyes narrowed, and his entire body tensed. "About eighteen months. You can go into the sitting room off the bedroom. Ms. Kloss is still packing, but I'll make sure she knows you're here. If you'll excuse me, I need to let the staff know and make preparations to shut down the house until things can be settled."

"I might need to ask you more questions," Jack said.

José nodded and reached into his pocket, pulling out a gold business card holder and flipping it open. "My information is on here if you need me."

He pointed us into the sitting room, and then went in another door farther down the hall.

"If looks could kill," I said, looking around the modern sitting room. Everything was white—carpet, furniture, walls—and I wondered if a room so white could really be lived in. Or maybe it was just me who needed décor that could camouflage the occasional spill or crumbs.

"Nice view," I said. There was a perfect view of the golf course and the swimming pool. "How come we don't have a pool?"

"Because I've never had time to swim," Jack said. "But if you promise to swim naked I'll promise to start making the time."

"I could agree to that if a hot tub is included."

"Deal," Jack said. "We can have one in before summer starts and kick things off with a party."

I squenched my nose. "On second thought…"

"Too late," he said, grinning. "What are your thoughts on José?

"I think there's no love lost between him and the girlfriend. His attitude shows she's not the boss. He reports to Donnelly alone."

"But if I'm reading him right," Jack said, "I don't think there's any love lost between José and Donnelly either. He's loyal. But there's resentment there."

The inner door to the sitting room was flung open and whom I could only assume was Kimberly Kloss came in with a flair I had to appreciate. She barely looked old enough to vote, and the thought of her and Donnelly together made my lip curl involuntarily in disgust.

Kimberly Kloss was about five foot ten, and built like a Victoria's Secret model. Her breasts were manmade and her hips nonexistent. Her hair was white blond and pulled into a high ponytail that trailed down her back. She wore black leather pants and a red sweater that wouldn't have kept anyone warm, considering the designer had forgotten to put material on the front and back.

The angry expression on her face smoothed out when she took her first look at Jack.

"Well, hello," she said. "You've caught me at a bad time. Maybe we could make an appointment and meet again another time. I'm about to leave on vacation. Though I wouldn't mind packing you in my suitcase."

I was guessing Donnelly's interest in her was purely physical, because if I had to listen to that voice all day I'd run screaming off the top of a building.

"I'm Sheriff Lawson, and my wife prefers I take my vacations with her," he said smoothly.

"Pity," she said. "I've found wives come and go."

"Not his," I said, taking a step forward.

She arched a finely sculpted brow and pouted her lips. "Whatever," she said. "Is this about my parking tickets? I don't have time for this. Leave your card or whatever with José and someone will get back to you to pay them. My fiancé will be here any minute and then we're leaving."

She turned on her heel to walk back out when Jack interrupted her.

"Ms. Kloss, John Donnelly is dead," he said. "You're going to have to sit down and answer some questions for me."

She spun back around, her face leeching of all color, and I thought she might pass out. And then color rushed into her face until she looked like a teakettle about to boil over.

"Get out!" she screeched. "I don't know what kind of sick joke you're playing, but I don't have to tolerate this. I'll have you fired. Do you know who my fiancé is? Get out of my house!"

She took a step toward Jack with her claws out, and he braced himself for an attack. "Don't take another step toward me or you're going to regret it," he said, his voice level and calm. "You don't want to spend the night in jail on top of everything else. I suggest we sit down and talk things through before you end up in trouble."

Her steps faltered, and her gaze narrowed while she tried to decide if Jack was serious.

"I'm calling our lawyer," she said instead. "I know my rights."

"Clearly you don't," Jack said. "Because all I'm trying to do is give you the courtesy of knowing that the man you live with has been murdered. But by all means, if you'd like to call your attorney we can do this in a formal setting down at the sheriff's office."

"I don't like you," she said, crossing her arms over her chest.

"I don't care," Jack said. "Now sit down."

Jack's tone must have gotten through to her because her mouth clamped tight and she took a seat in the little white chair by the window.

"You're mistaken," she said, examining her lethal manicure. "John and I are scheduled to be on the five o'clock flight to Aruba. He wouldn't die right now. He wouldn't do that to me."

I raised a brow but said nothing. I'd never met John Donnelly in person, but I'd seen him in interviews on various networks. He had a forceful, larger than life personality, and he had the kind of charisma that could make you believe white was black, even if you were staring the proof in the face. I couldn't imagine what John Donnelly and Kimberly Kloss had in common, other than her love for his money, and his need for someone young and pretty to feed his ego.

"Ms. Kloss—"

"Kimmie," she interrupted. "Call me Kimmie."

"My name is Sheriff Lawson, and this is Dr. Graves. She's the coroner for the county. Mr. Donnelly has been dead two days. Is there a reason you didn't report him missing?"

Her eyes narrowed again, and I could tell she was getting all worked up. "You talked to José, right? I swear, I'm firing that bastard. I don't know who he thinks he is running his mouth to the cops."

"Why didn't you report him missing?" he asked again.

"Because he does this sometimes," she said between gritted teeth. "Just because José likes to have his nose up John's ass every second doesn't mean John doesn't need a little space now and then. I would too if that nosy son of a bitch kept track of me like that. It's no big deal. After John wins a case, he likes to unwind for a couple of days. He'll head over to the Judge's Chamber for a few drinks, and he'll usually buy a round for whoever's there, and then he kind of plays it by ear. Though I thought he'd come home since we're supposed to leave for our trip."

"Where does he stay when he doesn't come home?" Jack asked. "Have there been other women in the picture? A man like John Donnelly doesn't seem like the kind of man to go anywhere alone?"

"Where does he stay?" Jack asked. "Do you suspect another woman in the picture?"

Jack was baiting her, which was very unlike him, but I had to say I was enjoying it immensely. Whatever his reasons, it was very entertaining.

Kimmie stood up so abruptly she knocked over the chair. "How dare you? What did José tell you?" she asked. "José!" she yelled. "Get your scrawny ass in here." Then she started pacing in her skyscraper heels. "Sometimes he'd get a room at the Cromwell.

Sometimes he'd stay with a friend. He was *not* cheating on me, no matter what José says about Julie Burkett. They were together before we met. He ended it. End of story."

José took that inopportune moment to answer Kimmie's bellow, and she had those red nails extended and ready to launch in a flash.

"Sit!" Jack commanded, and then he looked at José and said, "I'll follow up with you later."

José nodded and ducked back out, but not before I saw the smirk on his face.

"I've had enough of your harassment," Kimmie hissed at Jack. "Consider your job gone by the time I get through talking to your boss."

"Maybe you didn't hear me say I'm the sheriff," Jack said, with more patience than I would've had at this point. "I am the boss. If you want to have me fired then vote in the next election. And if you don't start answering questions, I'm going to assume you have something to hide. John Donnelly was murdered. This is my last warning. So sit down and answer the questions."

She took a couple of steps backward until she realized she'd knocked the chair over, so she left it toppled and moved to its twin on the opposite side of the window.

"I didn't kill him," she said. "I would never do that. We were leaving for vacation. Why would I kill him and ruin our trip?"

"You don't seem very surprised he was murdered," I said.

"Are you kidding me?" she asked. "Everyone wanted to kill John. Even his friends. He got death threats all the time. He said powerful men were always a target, and that I'd just have to get used to it. I kind of freaked out a little because I saw this movie once where someone put a bomb under some mobster's wife's car and blew her to bits to teach her husband a lesson. But we've got real good security here, and we always park the cars in the garage."

"Any of the death threats stand out?" Jack asked.

You'd have to ask his secretary. Mary—Maggie—Martha. Something like that. She keeps a record of that stuff. The only recent one I know about is the delivery he got here a couple of weeks ago with a dead cat in it. I happened to be standing there when he opened the package. John doesn't want me to worry, so he doesn't like to bring the troubles from work home."

"Thoughtful of him," I said.

"But I couldn't help but see the cat. Its head had been cut off, and I think I screamed. I don't remember much after that. When I woke up it was gone. John gave me a sweet little diamond tennis bracelet to show how sorry he was I had to see something like that." She jiggled her wrist and diamonds flashed in the sunlight.

"When was the last time you saw him?" Jack asked.

She shrugged and moved to stand in front of the large mirror propped against the wall, checking her appearance. "I don't know. I got back from Paris Sunday, so I've been kind of jet-lagged and sleeping super late. He was finishing up a big trial Monday and Tuesday, so I didn't see him at all those days because he was working late, but he left a present for me on his pillow with a note Wednesday morning telling me to be ready to celebrate a big win."

"The same night as the storm hit," Jack said.

She leaned over in front of the mirror and plumped her breasts so her cleavage showed better, and then she dabbed at the corner of her mouth where her red lipstick had smeared. "Yeah, now that you mention it," she said. "I'd forgotten about that. I hate storms, so I took an Ambien and was out like a light. I didn't even know about the tornadoes until I was having a late lunch at the club the next day."

"Who was here with you in the house?" Jack asked.

"I don't know. The house is usually empty in the evenings. The staff only comes during the day, and on certain days of the week. Gardeners, pool guys, housekeepers. The cook comes in every day. And José goes off to his creepy apartment over the garage every night. God knows what he does over there. I was laying out by the pool one day and I looked up, and he was just standing in his window staring at me. I demanded John fire him right away, but John just laughed and told me that was the price of being beautiful.

"Did Mr. Donnelly ever talk to you about his health?" I asked.

Kimmie looked confused. "What do you mean?"

"He was sixty years old," I said. "Did he have any health problems that you noticed? Did he have regular doctor appointments?"

"I don't know," she said, shrugging. "He'd sometimes get dizzy. He said he'd get these little spots in front of his eyes, and then he'd have to lie down for a few minutes. I just figured he wanted me to pay a little more attention to him."

"It was most likely the lack of oxygen getting to his brain," I said dryly.

"We didn't really talk about that stuff," she said. "He seemed okay to me. Not like a regular sixty-year-old. Most of those guys are old and gross. But I had no idea John was as old as he was when we met. I thought he was in his forties. He was so sexy and commanding. And he never had to take those little pills or anything for sex.

"I noticed he started getting a little soft around the middle last year, but he'd play golf or racquetball at the club to let off steam. And he was trying to eat better, so he had Maria make low-calorie meals. And a drink every now and then never hurt anybody. The only thing I didn't like was those stinky cigars, but he'd go out on the terrace and smoke them. You couldn't ever tell John to do anything he didn't want to. He was ninety to nothing all the time. He never slowed down. I had to beg for months to get him to take this vacation. And now it's ruined."

"I'm sure they'd let you change your reservation to one," Jack said. "Or you could find a friend to go with you."

"You think?" she said, completely missing the sarcasm in Jack's tone.

"What about plastic surgery?" I asked. "Botox injections."

She waved a hand at that and said, "Oh, sure. Everybody does that. Dr. Park takes care of all that. Teddy Park. He and John play golf sometimes. They live directly across from us on the other side of the lake. John said appearances mean just as much in court as good storytelling. The jurors get bored if you don't keep them entertained."

"Our justice system at work," I said, looking at Jack.

"Thanks for your time," Jack said. "We'll be in touch if we have any other questions. I will ask that you not leave town until I've cleared you to go."

"I'll call the resort and have them change the reservation to next week. I'm sure you'll have it all wrapped up by then. What am I supposed to do about his body? When can I bury him? Who takes care of all that stuff?"

"I've got calls in to his children," Jack said. "They're the only next of kin I could find. I'll let you all know when we've released the body."

"Next of kin," she said, shaking her head. "I'm his fiancée. Those brats don't give a damn about John. But you can bet they'll be here to loot through the house and steal from me. I'm calling our attorney," she said, talking to herself more than us at this point. "This house and everything in it is mine. They'll have to pry it from my cold dead hands."

"That should be interesting," I said under my breath as Jack and I turned to leave.

"Let's get out of here," he said. "My ears are starting to bleed."

5

I WAS SURPRISED WHEN JACK TURNED BACK TOWARD the entrance gate rather than Dr. Park's home on the other side of the lake.

"Where are we going?" I asked.

"The Judge's Chamber," he said. "Kimmie said he'd head there after a big case. My guess is that's where the booze and bar mix you found in his stomach originated. We need a timeline, and to find who the last person to see him alive was."

"I feel like I need a shower," She was a real piece of...work," I said. "I've never seen you intentionally try to make someone angry like that. Interesting tactic. Or is that part of your reelection strategy?"

He grinned and accelerated into the turn. "Just wanted to push her buttons a little and see what kind of temperament she had. She's too hot-headed, too impulsive. Her emotions rule her. Whoever killed

John was cold and calculating. We'll check with José to see if he knows if what she said about taking a sleeping pill is true, but my gut says it probably is. She's selfish at heart. She wouldn't think twice about worrying whether or not he was out in the storm, or maybe lost or stranded. Her main concern is herself."

"You think she's right about the house and everything in it being hers?" I asked.

"I don't know," he said. "She wasn't wearing an engagement ring."

"I noticed," I said. "But she had plenty of other shiny baubles. All I know is that John Donnelly's will reading should be very interesting. Maybe we could get tickets to attend."

"If you wanted to go to the circus you should've said so," he said, cracking a smile. "You ever been to the Judge's Chamber?"

"Nah, it came along after my bar-hopping days," I said. "It's too far out, and word on the street is the cops like to set up checkpoints and bust people driving home.

"This town is lousy with cops," Jack said, laughing.

"Not to mention there are people there," I said. "And people generally want to strike up random conversations, most of which I care nothing about."

"You're such a people person," he said. "My wife, the Crypt-Keeper. Maybe that should be your Halloween costume."

I narrowed my eyes. "I said I would go. You're not putting me in a costume. There's nothing in the wife handbook about dressing up."

"That's not what you said the other night when you wore that red thing," he said.

"That wasn't a costume," I said, punching him in the shoulder. "That's an…accessory. Besides, I barely wore it."

"I remember," he said, clutching his hand to his heart. "You know if you dress in the right costume, no one will know who you are and they won't talk to you."

"Hmm," I said, thinking it over. He had a point. "Are you trying to trick me?"

"That's hurtful," he said. "I'd never do that."

"Uh-huh," I said, shifting things back on topic. "Tell me about the Judge's Chamber."

"It's a cop bar for the most part," he said. "But anyone who works for Lady Justice shows up there sooner or later—lawyers, social workers, civil service—everyone but you, apparently."

"I don't recall ever hearing you talk about hanging out there," I said.

"And me," he agreed. "Not my scene. Mike Costello owns the place."

"Why does that name sound familiar? Is he from Bloody Mary?"

"He was a cop," Jack said. "Left the force a year before I took over as sheriff. But I got to inherit the mess he left. Costello decided to relieve himself in an alley while on duty and a mugger decided to take advantage of the situation. The guy used Costello's weapon against him, and Costello ended up getting shot in the knee. Sheriff Drummond raked him over the coals and put him on leave, but Costello got to the media first and told his heroic side of the story. Guess who he told it to?"

I growled low in my throat. "Let me guess. Floyd Parker."

"Bingo. Floyd's article catches traction, and all of a sudden Costello's name is splashed across every media outlet, and at that point it doesn't matter what the truth is. The people have already decided Drummond screwed Costello over. Costello ends up suing the department for his own stupidity, and also played it up to the media how bad the crime is in King George for cops to get assaulted on the street. It wasn't a good year for Donald Drummond. It's the main reason why he lost the election against me."

"And the fact that Donald Drummond was an idiot," I said.

"That didn't help," Jack agreed. "But if Drummond had done a press conference as soon as Costello was suspended it would've been a very different story. But Drummond liked to keep things close to the vest in the department. It's why there was so much corruption to clean up when I got there."

"What'd you do with Costello?" I asked.

"We ended up settling just to get Costello to shut up, and he took early retirement. He'd been on the job just long enough to be vested. But I've never had much use for cops who do a half-assed job just hoping to pull in a pension at the end of their thirty years. Those kinds of cops aren't useful to anyone."

"And how does he feel about you?" I asked.

"I have no idea," he said. "I haven't seen or thought about him in more than a decade."

It took almost half an hour to get to the Judge's Chamber, and I was surprised to see so many cars in the parking lot.

"He's not doing a bad business," I said.

"He's killing it. He bought this place and all the land around it with his settlement money, then he turned around and sold most of the land to a developer for millions. This place will be breaking fire codes in the next few hours. It's Saturday night."

I groaned. I had no idea what day of the week it was. The days tended to blur from one to the next, especially when work was my focus. "I guess I can see why you wanted to do this now instead of waiting until after Dr. Park."

"I get a good idea every once in a while," he said. "Just a heads up, this is probably going to be very awkward."

"That's pretty much how my whole day has gone," I said, getting my first real look at the Judge's Chamber. It was built like a big barn with big timbers and a metal roof. "This place is huge."

I heard the music as soon as we got out of the Tahoe, and I was immediately thankful it was the canned kind and not a live band. I'd passed the age where I liked having my eardrums rung for no reason whatsoever.

I knew what awkward meant the second we walked through the doors. Everyone knew Jack. But Jack didn't spend his time in bars, especially bars where a group of his cops were sitting in a corner, and a group of defense attorneys those cops had most assuredly testified as expert witnesses against were sitting in the other.

"Hey, Sheriff," the cops called from the corner. I recognized everyone. I'd already seen Cole and Martinez that morning, and Durrant and Diaz were there as well.

"Pull up a chair," Cole said, tipping his beer in our direction. "We're just getting started. These slackers all have tomorrow off, so my night is going to be cut short since we're still working the scarecrow case we found this morning."

All the other officers worked four twelves since they were patrol cops, but Cole's scheduling was different since he was a detective and we were in the middle of a murder investigation. Generally speaking, there was no such thing as getting weekends off when murder was involved.

"I'm here to talk to Costello," Jack said. "But thanks for the invite."

Cole made a face at the mention of Costello's name. "I always hated that bastard ended up with this bar. But he serves cheap drinks."

"Amen for that," Martinez said.

"Any news on the ID of our vic yet?" Cole asked, tossing a couple of peanuts into his mouth.

"That's why I'm here to talk to Costello," Jack said. "The vic was John Donnelly."

The surprise at the whole table was palpable, and Cole muttered an expletive. "You've got to be shitting me."

"Why?" Jack asked.

"Because he was here," Durrant said. "Wednesday night. We saw him leave. He was drunk as two skunks. He couldn't even walk a straight line out the door. We figured the guys running the checkpoint out by Broken Bow would catch him."

Durrant reminded me of a beanpole. He was tall and skinny, and his face was long and narrow. He had puppy-dog-brown eyes and hair that never quite managed to stay out of his face. He and Martinez had been closest to Lewis, and I'd heard the rumors that they'd both been frequenting the bars more often since their friend had died. They wouldn't be the first cops who tried to ease their pain with alcohol, but it never led to anything but poor decisions, slower reaction times, and broken relationships.

Jack nodded. "Notice anything unusual?"

"The drinking was his usual," Cole said. "He's a regular. I don't come here that often, but he's almost always here somewhere between six and eight o'clock. Donnelly was a creature of habit. He always sat at that end seat of the bar, facing the door. He'd drink whiskey neat and talk to Costello until he could barely stay on his barstool. He gave us the stink eye on his way out, and that's the last time we saw him." Cole smiled grimly. "Hops and Chen were working the checkpoint that night. I'll ask them if they saw him pass. He drives that fancy red Porsche. It's kind of hard to miss."

"Good call," Jack said. "I want to talk to Costello before things get too crazy in here. Y'all be good."

"Always are," Martinez said.

Jack clapped him on the shoulder, and we turned toward the bar. I knew Jack was worried about Martinez. He and Lewis had been tight, and losing a partner is like losing a member of your family. Jack had required all the officers that had been involved in the incident with my parents to undergo mandatory counseling. Even with the counseling, it was something they'd live with and have nightmares about for the rest of their lives. I knew this from experience. I'd been having nightmares about my parents ever since my dad had come back from the dead.

I'd noticed the man behind the bar hadn't taken his eyes off us since we walked in. He'd tended to his customers and made small talk, but his attention was for us alone. I could only assume this was Mike Costello. He reminded me of a hairy garden gnome, and I couldn't ever imagine him putting on the uniform. But his eyes told a different story. Cop eyes were always recognizable.

"Costello," Jack said, moving to the end of the bar where there were no people to overhear our conversation.

"Sheriff," Costello said. His tone wasn't friendly or unfriendly, just matter of fact. "First time I've seen you in here." He didn't seem too excited by the idea

"I'm here about John Donnelly," Jack said. "He's dead."

Costello tossed a wet rag onto the bar and said, "Aw, hell. I had a feeling something was wrong. Come on into the back where we can hear ourselves think." Costello grabbed a beer from the ice and yelled, “Sheree! Come tend the bar for me.”

We followed him into a small office area that smelled vaguely of lemons and old cigarettes. Costello plopped into a rolling chair with a squeaky wheel and gestured for us to sit in the two folding chairs against the wall. He took a long sip of the beer.

“We haven’t met,” Costello said, eyeing me up and down rudely.

“Dr. Graves,” I said, arching a brow. “County coroner.”

“Sure,” he said, dismissing me. “Saw your wedding picture in the paper. Heard an awful lot about you.”

Costello smirked and I knew whatever he’d heard had probably come from Floyd. I felt Jack tense beside me, but there was no change in his expression.

“You knew Donnelly?” Jack asked.

“Sure,” Costello said. “Closest thing to a friend that bastard probably ever had. It was rare I’d go more than two nights without seeing him unless he was out of town. I knew something was wrong when he didn’t show up last night. I think he was leaving on some trip today.”

“Yeah, Aruba,” Jack said. “He was here Wednesday night?”

Costello nodded. "He came in a little after five when he got done with court. Was raining cats and dogs out, so the crowd was light. Just my regulars. Stayed till a little after eight thirty. I shooed everyone home by nine and locked up because of the tornado warnings in the area. Barely made it home before things got real bad."

"Anything seem off about Donnelly?"

"Nah, nothing much shook John. He was anxious to get home to his woman. Was in a celebratory mood if you get my drift. He'd won a big case that day. He bought a couple of bottles of bubbly to take home to that infant he's seeing." Costello shuddered. "Hell, I don't even know if she's old enough to drink." Costello shuddered. "She's younger than my daughter. But with John's money, he never had problems getting tail. He's probably got another lined up for when he decides to move this one out."

"I thought they were getting married?" I asked.

Costello laughed so hard he had to wipe the tears from his eyes. "What in the Sam Hill gave you that idea? John would've slit his own wrists before he ever got married again."

"She seemed to think they were getting married," I said. "She said she was his fiancée."

"In her dreams," Costello said. "Literally. Because I can guarantee you John never brought up the word *marriage* to her. In fact, the more a woman starts hinting toward marriage, the faster he rushes them out the door."

"What about Julie Burkett?" Jack asked. "Know anything about her?"

"Sure, I know Julie," he said, the look in his eyes calculating. "She came in a few times with John. Nice lady. Too good for John, and he knew it. It's why he ended things."

"Were they still sleeping together?"

Costello shrugged. Who the hell cares? He'd crash at her place from time to time. Who knows if they were doing the nasty. That's between them. I'm a bartender. Not a priest."

"He didn't mention any trouble he was having?" Jack asked. "Anyone who was bothering him? Any threats?"

"Not recently," Costello said. "Not recently. Look, John wasn't a likable fellow. In fact, he had a way of drawing out the worst in people. It was a gift. At least in the courtroom. He could make a Sunday school teacher want to stab him in the heart. He's had plenty of threats. Had his tires slashed a couple of times, and a brick thrown through his office window. Things like that."

"So he's not exactly on everyone's Christmas card list," I said, making Costello chuckle.

"You got cameras in the parking lot?" Jack asked.

"Sure," he said. "You're welcome to the feed. I don't like the thought of someone doing this on my property. But the rain was so bad I'd be surprised if you could see anything. He parked right in front, over on the right side. I could see his headlights light up the window before he pulled out."

"His tox report came back with a blood alcohol level of .16," I said.

"Yeah, John liked the whiskey. But he's John, so you can't tell him what to do. He wouldn't listen. He never worried much about DWIs because he could buy his way out of any situation. Or make the one giving him trouble wish they were dead. But I am surprised he never wrapped any of his fancy toys around a telephone pole."

"Anyone off the top of your head you can think of that caused him more trouble than others?" Jack asked.

Costello thought for a minute. "Said he got a dead animal in the mail a couple of weeks ago, but didn't have a name to go with it. The only person I can think of who's been giving him real grief was the DA. Keeps trying to get him on ethics violations. And failing."

That was an interesting bit of information. And something I was hoping we wouldn't have to get entangled in. Because pissing off the DA was the equivalent of shooting yourself in the foot. It would hurt like hell and leave you with a permanent limp.

Not something Jack needed with an election coming up.

"Did Donnelly ever mention his health?" I asked. "Mention any doctors he was seeing?"

"No, but I told him he needed to go and get a physical. He wasn't looking good. Had that gray color to his face. I mentioned once that maybe he should cut back on the booze, but he just laughed it off and told me to pour him another drink. He said he was the kind of guy that both heaven and hell didn't want, so he figured he was destined to live forever."

"Guess he was wrong," I said. "He had lung cancer. Pretty advanced. And his heart and liver were both ticking time bombs. I would've been surprised if he'd lasted another six months."

"Doesn't make him any less murdered," Costello said.

"No," I agreed. "What about the plastic surgery?"

Costello chuckled. "His body might have been shit on the inside, but he always made sure it was packaged well. Said appearances were everything."

"Thanks for your time," Jack said. "If I can just get the camera feed."

"I'll copy it to a disc for you," Costello said. "Security feed is in here." He opened a narrow door into what looked to be a large closet, but it was lined with TV monitors showing all the different camera feeds from around the property. I was surprised how good the quality was. Most businesses didn't bother to go so high end, making it almost impossible to get a visual on suspects when there was trouble.

"I heard Floyd Parker tossed his name in the ring for sheriff," Costello said, making the copy, along with small talk.

"That's what I heard," Jack said.

"Should be an interesting race," he continued. "I don't think you've had any real competition since your first term. He might throw a real wrench in the works for you."

"Could be," Jack said, not rising to the bait.

"Heard you assaulted him a few months back," he said, hoping to do the same to me. "I'm sure that's going to come up during the election."

"No," I said, shaking my head. "There was no assault on my end. In fact, Floyd impeding an investigation is on record since there were news cameras there at the time. Guess you got bad information."

"Guess so," he said, handing Jack the disc. "Well, the bar keeps me busy. But I like to support candidates from time to time. Keeps me entertained in my retirement."

"We all have to have a hobby," Jack said. "Thanks for your time. And the disc."

The corner table was empty when we came out, and Costello's mouth tightened at the lost revenue. I waited to speak until we were outside.

"Did I just understand him right that he's going to put money behind Floyd Parker in the election?" I asked.

"That's how I took it," Jack said calmly. "Makes sense to me. Floyd helped Costello out by writing that article, and now it's time for payback.

There was a door on each side of the vestibule, and Jack took the one on the right, heading toward the area where Costello said Donnelly's car had been parked.

"I don't like to talk bad about people," I said, making Jack snort. "But if he's hanging out with guys like John Donnelly and supporting jerkwads like Floyd Parker, then I'm going to have to use all your money to make sure he comes out on the losing end. Maybe we could buy his bar and set it on fire. Or check to see if he owes back taxes."

Jack pulled me close and kissed the top of my head. "I'm glad you're on my side. And I'm going to pretend I didn't hear you say that about burning down the bar."

Something crunched under my feet and I looked down at the shards of glass on the sidewalk. And then I took a closer look. It was starting to get dark, so I used the flashlight on my phone.

"There's the rest of it," Jack said, pointing to the larger pieces mixed in with the dirt and mulch of the flower bed. "Someone must have kicked it out of the way."

"It's a champagne bottle," I said. "Or what's left of one."

"Yeah, an expensive one," Jack said, recognizing the label. "I've got an evidence bag in the car. Let's get what we can."

"Grab a few of them," I said. "There are some cigarette butts too."

Jack was back in a hurry and we brushed the shards and pieces into an evidence bag, and also came up with three cigarette butts and a piece of chewing gum.

"The last window of the restaurant is here," Jack said, "So he wouldn't have been parked any farther down the row and his lights still flashed in the window. There's a camera on the corner, and there was another over the entry door to see people coming in and out."

"Hopefully we can get a good shot of Donnelly on the disc. You think someone got him here and drove the car away?" I asked.

"He was drunk," Jack said. "This would be the easiest time to do it. It was already raining. Visibility was low. It was dark. All it would take was a quick blow to the head and a shove into the car. It wouldn't have taken long."

"Blows to the head is consistent with the autopsy report. He was hit hard. Maybe more than once. It was definitely hard enough to give him a concussion."

"The car should be in impound by tomorrow morning. We'll have the team go through it and see if there's blood or anything else. You up for one more stop?"

"Do I get tacos?" I asked.

"I feel like you asking the question is actually giving me a choice in the matter. I appreciate that."

"I do what I can," I said. "But seriously. Tacos first. Then the stop. Where are we going, by the way?"

"It seems like a good time to pay Julie Burkett a visit," he said.

"You think she's going to be home on a Saturday night?"

"Don't you like to stay home on Saturday nights?"

"Always. I'd much rather go out on a weeknight. Less people. Less traffic."

"Maybe Julie Burkett feels the same way."

"Maybe," I said. "Just don't forget the tacos."

6

Julie Burkett's house was on the way to Bloody Mary. She lived in a nice neighborhood, with small, single-story houses that each had a single tree planted in the front yard. Cars were parked along the street and porch lights were on.

Number 802 had a white SUV in the driveway and hanging plants on the porch. Jack parked in front of the house instead of the driveway. The neighbors on one side of Julie's house were sitting on the front porch laughing, and I could hear the television from inside the house on the other side.

Julie's front door was open, but the screen door was latched. Jack knocked and we waited for someone to come to the door.

The woman who unlatched the screen wasn't the kind of woman I'd been expecting. She was in her fifties, and her dark hair was naturally streaked with silver. Her face was free of makeup, and she had creases at the corner of her eyes that said she laughed often.

"Can I help you?" she asked.

"I'm Sheriff Lawson," Jack said, showing her his badge. "And this is Dr. Graves. We need to speak to you for a few minutes. It's about John Donnelly."

Her mouth opened in surprise, but she closed it quickly and nodded, stepping out of the way so we could come inside. The entryway was the size of a postage stamp, but it opened into a larger living area that was comfortably furnished with bold colors and interesting art on the walls. There was no television, but there was an antique gramophone in the corner.

"You're Julie Burkett?" Jack asked.

"Yes," she said. "I'm sorry. I guess I'm a little flustered. Is everything okay? Please sit down. I can make some tea."

"We're fine, Ms. Burkett," Jack said, taking a seat on the couch next to me. "But I'm sorry to tell you that John Donnelly's body was found yesterday morning. He was murdered."

Other than the slight widening of her eyes, it was as if we hadn't spoken. It was several moments before she said anything. "I don't understand. That can't be." She had the glazed look of someone in shock, and then she seemed to shake herself and straighten her spine. "That fool. I told him he needed to be more careful. Death threats are nothing to ignore."

"What was your relationship with John?" Jack asked.

She curled her legs up under her in the chair and smiled slightly. There was grief in her eyes. Real grief. Raw.

"Oh, well," she said. "I'm guessing you already have an idea of that or you wouldn't be here. John and I were complicated. He was a difficult man. A demanding man. A heartless one as well. He had vices and faults. He was a womanizer and greedy and selfish. He fought for the wrong side, and he rarely had a conscience about it. But I saw the potential in him. For a time he tried to change. To be a different man. He was a man I loved. But ultimately, he just wasn't good for me and I had to break free."

"But you still had a relationship," Jack said.

She nodded her head. "I wouldn't call it a relationship. Not anymore. A decade ago I almost married him. He made promises. And I really do think he loved me. At least as much as he knew how to love. But I told him I couldn't go through with it. He was angry for a time, and we didn't speak for almost two years. But then we ran into each other at a wine tasting and struck up a conversation. One thing led to another. But I had boundaries in place, to protect my heart this time.

"He'd come and go, in and out of my life as he pleased. I wouldn't allow him to buy me gifts or trinkets or take me places. I didn't want anything from him but him. The real him. And if he wanted to spend time with me he was always welcome here. How was he killed?"

"He had a heart attack," I said. "The trauma of being abducted was too much strain on his heart." I felt it best to leave out the torture.

She sighed. "His health was bad. We both knew his time was limited. It wasn't too long ago the doctor gave him the news."

"Do you know which doctor?" Jack asked.

"I'm sorry, no. He never mentioned a name. But I know he was working to get all his affairs in order."

"When was the last time you saw him?" Jack asked.

"He stayed here Monday and Tuesday night," she said. "It's not far from his office and he was working late on a case, so he swung by here instead of driving all the way home."

"Did you expect to see him again this week?"

"No, actually," she said. "He was scheduled to go on a trip to Aruba. John hates the beach. Detests it. But I told him to stop complaining and go try to make something of his ridiculous relationship with that girl."

"It didn't bother you he was in a relationship with someone else?" I asked.

Julie looked at me with steady green eyes. "He was always in a relationship with someone else. And no, it didn't bother me. I accepted John for who and what he was. He was never mine. But I'll miss him. He was a great conversationalist with a quick wit and sharp mind."

"Can you give me your whereabouts Wednesday night and Thursday during the day?" Jack asked.

"Hmm," she said, reaching for her phone on the table beside her and scrolling through her calendar. "I teach art classes on Wednesday nights at the civic center," she said. "But they shut things down early because of the storm and I drove straight home. I got here in time to get all my hanging baskets off the porch and inside.

"Thursday I taught back-to-back yoga classes at the Y, and I had lunch with my mother. Can you let me know about the arrangements for his funeral?" she asked.

"We can," Jack said. "Thank you for your time. It's been very enlightening."

"Enlightening?" I asked as we got back in the car. "More like confusing. Are we sure she's talking about the same John Donnelly everyone else loves to hate?"

"No one can change a man like the woman he loves," Jack said.

We were just pulling out of the neighborhood when Cole called. "Hey, Sheriff," he said. "I got in touch with Hops and Chen, and neither of them saw a red Porsche heading past the checkpoint on Broken Bow."

"Good to know," Jack said, "which means he went the other direction. Maybe once we get some more information we'll be able to pinpoint a location for the murder."

Jack stayed on the phone for most of the drive home, getting updates about areas that were still without power, citizens who had major property damage, and an updated body count. The body count was up to eight. Two more had just been found who had only been missing up to now—a man and his six-year-old daughter.

When he hung up the phone I said, "Are we calling it a night? You look like you could use a solid twelve."

He laughed and rubbed at his eyes. "I look that good, huh? The tacos helped. I've got lots of energy now."

"Tacos can do that to a man," I said.

"I just want to be home. I can barely remember what the inside of the house looks like."

"Just so you know," I said. "I haven't been to the grocery store. There's no food in the house for tomorrow."

"That's okay. My mom texted and said she put a lasagna in the oven for us, and a salad in the fridge."

"God bless your mother," I said, my mouth watering.

I'd known Jack's mom my whole life, and she'd been more of a mother to me growing up than my own had ever been. Which makes complete sense now that I knew my mom had been a double agent working for the CIA. Motherly she definitely was not.

We were still in King George Proper and about to cross into Bloody Mary when Jack swore, and the sound of gunfire had me sitting up in my seat.

"You've got to be kidding me," Jack said, hitting his sirens.

It took me a minute to see what Jack had seen in an instant. There was a lone man running out of the convenience store with a pistol in one hand and cartons of cigarettes in the other. One of the county units was parked to the side of the building, and the officer had been inside.

"Call it in," Jack said, and hit the ground running.

My heart was beating a million miles per minute, but I did as I was told and called in to dispatch.

“Dispatch,” I said. “This is Dr. Graves. Robbery in progress. Shots fired.” I rattled off the name of the store and location.

I’d lost the visual of Jack. Officer Plank had come out the front of the convenience store seconds after Jack had started chasing the man, and then they’d all disappeared down the alley. I reached over and pulled Jack’s door closed and locked myself in, and then I checked in the glove box for a backup weapon.

Jack was one of those people who had backup weapons everywhere. I’d found one under the seat cushion in the living room and another in the canister labeled *flour*. There was one taped behind the toilet in our bathroom, and another hidden under the cup towels. And thank God Jack was a creature of habit because there was a snub nose revolver and a taser in his glove box.

I checked to make sure the revolver was loaded, and checked the battery on the taser. I could hear sirens in the background, growing closer with every second, and my only solace was that no more shots had been fired.

Something hard hit the side of my door, and someone was jerking at the handle, trying to open it. His eyes were wild and rolling, and it was obvious he was high on something. I couldn’t help the yelp of surprise that left my mouth as he smashed the butt end of his gun against the window, causing it to shatter.

"Get out of the car!" he yelled.

I was covered in glass, but I saw him raise the gun and instinct took over. I pressed the taser to his forehead and he went down like a bag of cement.

I opened the door and got out of the car in a hurry, keeping the revolver pointed at him. If he was as drugged as I thought he was, he probably wouldn't stay down long. And he'd just get up mad. Jack and Plank skidded to a halt next to the robber, both of them winded. Plank knelt down and hurriedly put cuffs on him.

"Is he alive?" I asked.

"Yeah," Plank said, feeling his pulse. "He's alive. Holy cow, he was a fast little bugger. There's no way we would've caught him. Whatever he was on was making him fly."

"You scared me to death," Jack said, pulling me close. "I saw him break the window and I thought it was over. Then I see your hand pop out and blast him in the face. Are you cut?"

I looked down and saw the glitter of glass stuck in the folds of my shirt and in my hair. "No, I don't think so. Is anyone else hurt?"

"No," Plank said. "He didn't hit anything inside but a case of beer and the ATM. And here I thought I'd stop and grab a couple of hot dogs for dinner on my way home from shift. Never did get my dogs, but this is going to be a great story to tell at the station tomorrow."

I groaned. I'd never worked with Plank on any of my homicides. He was still a rookie. But I'd seen him around a time or two. He had the face of a cherub and didn't look old enough to vote. His skin was baby smooth, and there were two patches of red on his cheeks from the exertion.

"You were going to eat gas station hot dogs?" I asked, raising a brow. "You got a death wish?"

He grinned, showing a dimple in his cheek. "Hey, they make 'em good here. You should try one. They've even got a big crockpot of chili cooking off to the side for chili dogs."

"Good Lord," Jack said. "To be young and dumb again."

"I'm going to have to pass on all of it," I said. "But I'll know what COD to look for if you ever show up in my lab."

He chuckled, and then he and Jack hauled the perp up by the arms, and half carried, half dragged him to Plank's cruiser.

"All I wanted was my dogs and to go home and turn on the game. Now I've got to take this yahoo and get him booked, and I get to do all the paperwork that goes with it."

"That's the breaks, kid," Jack said, watching as two other units pulled into the lot with lights and sirens blaring. "But I bet if you ask nice, Wachowski will take him in and book him for you. She's got a sweet spot for you."

"Oh, yeah?" Plank asked, eyeing Wachowski from across the lot. "Maybe I could offer to buy her dinner as payback."

"As long as it's not gas station chili dogs that might be a good idea," Jack said. "I've heard Wachowski enjoys the occasional baseball game and beer."

"Even better. Thanks, Sheriff," he said. The red in his cheeks deepened, and I shook my head.

"That poor kid will never be able to get away with anything. I didn't realize you'd added matchmaker to your duties."

JACK GRINNED. "I just gave him a push. They've been mooning over each other since he got out of the academy three months ago."

"Mooning?" I asked. "Okay, Grandpa."

"Shut up," he said and swatted me on the butt.

A news van pulled into the lot just as Jack finished clearing out the broken glass from my seat. He returned the revolver and taser to the glove box and turned in time to see Carrie Colson stick a microphone in his face.

"Sheriff Lawson," she said, her smile blindingly white. "Can you give us an update of what happened here tonight?"

Jack was good at his job. People liked him and he had a charm about him that appealed to viewers. I took a step back out of the way so the spotlight was only on him. And then I heard her ask if he was worried about the rise in crime so close to the election.

"I wouldn't say a single incident resulting in someone's poor decisions is a rise in crime," Jack said, his smile firmly in place. "An officer was on site and he kept the workers and civilians safe by apprehending the suspect. My officers do a good job in keeping this county safe."

"What can you tell us about the murder of John Donnelly?" she asked. "My sources tell me his body was discovered yesterday at the Cotton farm, and he sustained a significant amount of torture."

"That investigation is still ongoing, but we're doing everything we can to find who's responsible. Thanks, Carrie," he said, and moved out of view of the camera to signal the interview was over.

Jack nodded at me and I hurried over to get into the Tahoe while Jack walked around to get in on his side. We didn't speak again until we were comfortably out of range.

"I'm glad you didn't shoot him," he said. "The paperwork would've gone on for years."

"And it would've made a great headline for Floyd to use against you. *Sheriff's Wife in Drug-Related Shootout.*"

I saw the corner of Jack's lip twitch as we headed toward home. We'd only had a slight detour, and I was hoping the lasagna was still warm.

I didn't feel myself relaxing until we turned onto Heresy Road and headed toward the house. Despite the fact it had been anything but a safe haven a few months ago when my father had decided to remove a couple of walls with an explosion that had almost cost us our lives—it *had* cost Lewis his—and I tried not to think about it every time the house came into view.

It had been my mother who'd taken my father's life. She'd been a double agent for the CIA the entire time, and her death two years before had been as fake as my father's. The life I'd known had been a lie, but my stability came with Jack. He was my family. He always had been. I no longer had to worry about my father. My mother had crawled back under whatever covert rock she was working under. And our lives had relatively returned to normal.

And though I'd hated the months of constant construction to fix the house, it hadn't been all bad. I'd gotten to make some decisions on colors, flooring, and furniture, which made it feel more like *our* house than me just moving into Jack's house after we'd gotten married.

We turned into the driveway and the three-story log structure came into view. The exterior lights were on, and so were the new lights that had been set up around the perimeter for security. I'd always loved Jack's house, even before we'd married. It was surrounded by towering pines, and the rough timbers on the outside blended in with the landscape.

"Please tell me you're not going to have to go back in tonight," I said, thinking about the lasagna, a glass of wine, and the possibility of a bath for two. The tacos had been more of an appetizer, and I felt like I'd burned a lot of calories back at the gas station. The adrenaline was starting to wane, and I knew from experience I'd either fall asleep where I was standing or I'd have more energy than I knew what to do with.

"I'm not going anywhere tonight," he said. "The guys have this one covered, the power company is still working on the downed lines. And everyone has finally been accounted for who was missing after the storm. You're thinking about the lasagna, aren't you?"

"You know me well," I said.

"Then I suggest we get food and wine, and call it a night."

I was a little disappointed. I'd been hoping we could connect in other ways, but I understood how tired he was, though maybe I'd earned a few extra points with my French toast-making skills that morning.

He parked the Tahoe in the garage since the window was missing, and we headed to the front door.

"Come on," I said. "You're asleep on your feet. We'll eat quick."

He unlocked the door and pushed it open, and the lights came on automatically when we walked across the threshold. Jack dumped his keys in the carved wooden bowl on the entry table.

I made a very unladylike sound as I was scooped up and tossed over Jack's shoulder.

"What are you doing?"

"I didn't say anything about going to sleep," he said, smacking me on the behind. "I just said we should call it a night. I hope you don't mind cold lasagna."

"I love it," I said.

I FELT like I'd been run over by a Mack truck the next morning. It was Sunday, and I was hoping Reverend Thomas would understand why we'd be missing morning services. Not that I was going to tell him. He'd probably be more understanding about Jack's insane work schedule for the week instead of the fact that I was too tired from a night of debauchery. Though I'm not sure married sex counted as debauchery. Unless you were married to Jack.

I was on my second cup of coffee and my eyes hadn't uncrossed yet. I tried not to let it show on my face because Jack's ego was big enough as it was, but he smirked every time he looked at me, so I could only guess I was failing.

"Want breakfast?" he asked.

I grunted. "And stop smirking. Nobody likes a show-off." I refilled my coffee cup from the carafe he'd sat in front of me.

"You're going to need your strength today," he continued, irritatingly cheerful. Jack was what I liked to call "a morning person." His eyes were bright from the second they opened, and his mouth opened not long after. I had no idea what happened from the time he closed his eyes at night to when he woke the next morning, but he always had something to say. I was the opposite of Jack. I couldn't form actual words for at least an hour after I woke up.

"I'm so glad you asked why," Jack said, putting fat slabs of bacon on to fry. "I keep thinking about how the body was posed. I want to run like crimes through the FBI database and see if we get a hit."

That got my attention. "You think the killer is a pro?"

"I think this wasn't his first kill," Jack said. "I combed through your report early this morning. Things like the heavy-gauge wire and the use of a cattle prod are different enough. But the way he was posed…"

I stayed silent. Jack wasn't really talking to me. He was thinking it through out loud. "The positioning of the body," he said. "It's almost a Christlike pose, like on the cross. If I remember my Bible history correctly, Judas Iscariot bought a field and hanged himself there after he betrayed Jesus for thirty pieces of silver."

"The Field of Blood," I said.

Jack nodded and poured pancake batter on the griddle. "Exactly. He hanged himself, and as he hung in the sunlight, it says his body burst and all his guts spilled out onto the field. Seems a little too coincidental since he was gutted postmortem."

"Reverend Thomas would be proud of you," I said. "You're probably the only person who makes it through his sermons without falling asleep."

He grinned and said, "John Donnelly is a traitor in many people's books. We just need to find out who he kissed on the cheek and betrayed."

"I'm going to assume you're going to call Carver," I said. "I'm sure he'll be thrilled. Michelle said he's driving her crazy working from home. Apparently, he talks constantly."

"He'll be back behind a desk in his office in another couple of weeks," Jack said.

Ben Carver was Jack's best friend, and he technically worked for the FBI, even though he was kind of an entity unto himself. He didn't really have a boss, and he wasn't really required to follow the rules. I had no idea what his title was, but he could get just about any piece of information, no matter how small, on just about anyone in the world. Which was terrifying, and why I was glad he was our friend and not our enemy.

Carver had been another victim of my father's crimes, and he was lucky to be alive. He'd had been run off the road and a tree had stopped his fall on the way into a ravine. Just about everything in Carver's body had been broken, and it had taken months of surgeries and rehabs before he'd been released to go home. He still had surgeries and rehab ahead of him, probably years of both, but he was alive, and he'd managed to keep all his limbs. More importantly, he'd managed to keep his brain despite the scare that he'd have permanent damage. Carver's brain was a thing to behold.

Jack put a plate in front of me, and I almost wept at the smell. I stopped just long enough to douse everything in syrup before I shoved food into my mouth.

"How did I get so lucky?" I asked around a bit of pancake. "You cook, you're good looking, and you have premium bedroom skills. I feel like a real slacker."

Jack's lips twitched. "You are. But I love you anyway."

I grinned, feeling much more alert. I was already thinking about taking up where we'd left off the night before.

"I can never tell if it's food or sex that puts that look in your eye," Jack said, sitting across from me with his own plate.

"Could be both," I said around a bite of pancake, "But this time it's sex."

"Good to know. We can multitask in the shower before I call Carver. I need to go into the station this morning and check on things. It must've been a full moon or something last night. The criminals were out in full force. Car theft, attempted burglary, shots fired by some drunk moron in his backyard, and three domestic disputes, one of which ended up with a woman in the hospital with multiple broken bones, and Officer Hops in the ER with eighteen stitches to the side of her eye where she got clocked with a broken vase."

"Wowza," I said. "Maybe Cole was right. We had a reprieve from crime the last couple of months and now it's payback time."

Jack groaned. "Don't say that. Cops are a superstitious lot. Last time we had a rash of crimes, Smith wore a garlic necklace for a month and Walters stopped changing his socks. It's just the season. Halloween seems to bring out the crazy in people. Just like Christmas. Crime always spikes around those holidays."

We finished breakfast, and I somehow managed to find the energy to stay upright while we multitasked in the shower. By the time we got out and dressed, my coffee had kicked in and my brain was functioning on all cylinders. I felt like I could conquer the world.

I gathered up all the dirty clothes and headed to the laundry room while Jack followed behind me with the phone, waiting for Carver to pick up. I was full of energy and feeling very domestic.

"If it isn't my favorite crime-fighting duo," Carver said by way of greeting.

"I thought Batman and Robin were your favorite," I said, dumping the clothes in the washing machine. I heard something rattle and then dug around in the machine until I extracted extra bullets that Jack had put in his pocket. I gave him a look and he shrugged. I'd washed some weird things since we'd been married. Who'd have known life as a cop's wife could be so exciting.

"I just like the costumes," Carver said. "Sometimes I dress up as Batman for Michelle. She likes to be Robin. That's how we ended up with Iris."

Iris was their infant who'd been born while Carver was still in the hospital.

"Lies!" I heard Michelle yell through the phone.

I chuckled. Carver and Michelle always brightened up my day.

"What have you got for me?" Carver asked. "I'm assuming you didn't just call to talk. You never do that. You're a texter. I enjoy your memes by the way. Very clever. But you only call when you have a case you need my help with."

Jack had known Carver a lot longer than I had, but we both knew the best way to deal with him was to let him wind down on his own. He'd eventually run out of steam.

"So..." Carver finally said. "What's up?"

"Got called to a scene yesterday morning," Jack said. "The victim was male, early sixties. And he was strung up on a scarecrow pole in the middle of a farmer's field. The killer spilled his guts postmortem."

"Ah, like Judas Iscariot," Carver said.

"Wow, that was a fast Bible reference," I said.

"Altar boy," he said. "You'll probably find the victim was seen as a betrayer of some kind, either in his profession or a business deal. Something along those lines."

"Attorney," Jack said. "John Donnelly. He's been on the news recently."

"I don't watch the news," Carver said. "It makes my blood pressure go up. I can find better fiction on Netflix. We've been watching a lot of *The Magic School Bus*. That Ms. Frizzle is a real pistol."

"Donnelly definitely fits your description," Jack said, getting the conversation back on track. "He's got a reputation for getting criminals off. The wealthy kind. He's brilliant at finding loopholes, and juries love him. There are a lot of terrible people walking free right now because of that man."

"You'll need to go through case files," Carver said. "A guy like that is sure to get some threats."

"We'll meet with his secretary tomorrow," Jack said. "Jaye finished the autopsy and the guy was extensively tortured. He's got burn marks from what looks like a cattle prod. Lots of broken bones, kneecaps, fingers—the usual stuff that indicates torture. Broken ribs too."

"One of his eyes was missing," I said, cutting in. "The body had some scavenger damage so I wasn't sure if it had been done by an animal or the killer, but I found evidence of a straight-edged cut around the eye socket."

"An eye for an eye?" Carver asked.

"Possibly," Jack said, meeting my gaze. "The killer also used a heavy-gauge wire to tie the victim to the scarecrow pole, and a natural-fiber rope to restrain the victim when he was being tortured. I've got Cole doing a search for the two items purchased together, but they're both fairly common. We thought you could run like crimes and see if anything popped, either for how the body was left for us to find or any of the materials used."

"I can do that," he said. "Shouldn't take too long at all. I already beat my new video game, and I think Magnolia has PMS. She's been very moody today."

Carver's relationship with his computers was legendary, if not a little creepy. He had a closer relationship to the "women" in his life, as he liked to call them, than most men had with their wives. When I'd first met Carver, his special lady was Matilda. Then he moved onto Miranda, but she'd been stolen in the car wreck that had almost taken his life. But Carver was no dummy when it came to his computers. No one could access them but him, and anyone who did was met with an unpleasant surprise, so Miranda had self-detonated.

He'd mourned Miranda longer than seemed reasonable, in my opinion, but Carver's nephew Doug, who was a lot like his uncle, came up with the name Magnolia for his new computer. According to Carver, she was a cross between Dixie Carter and Scarlett O'Hara.

Carver's wife didn't seem to be bothered by his relationship with Magnolia. The last time I'd talked to her she'd told me if Magnolia was real, she would've baked her a cake for keeping him occupied. Carver was driving Michelle crazy. She was an attorney working from home so she could take care of her husband and four girls, one of which was a newborn.

"If Magnolia is up to it, we'd appreciate the help," Jack said. "I'm still dealing with tornado cleanup."

"Michelle told me you guys got hit pretty hard," he said. "Any casualties?"

"Eight total," Jack said. "Just found the final missing two yesterday."

"Sorry to hear that. I'm going to try and sweet-talk Magnolia into letting me stroke her keys. A little sweet talk always works with Michelle."

"No, it doesn't!" I heard her yell again.

I laughed outright this time.

"Don't encourage her," Carver said. "I'm lucky she hasn't slit my throat. Having six people on lockdown in the same house is a challenge. Mostly for her. I'll get back to you soon. Whoever your killer is probably won't be satisfied with playing God just once."

"That was our thought too," Jack said and disconnected.

I followed him back downstairs, and watched him strap on his weapon, and then the backup around his ankle. There was something about the routine that I found comforting.

"I shouldn't be gone too long," he said. "An hour, maybe two. I'm going to leave the Tahoe with maintenance so they can fix the window, and I'll get one of the guys to bring me home. I want to check on Hops while I'm out, and make sure she's okay. Eighteen stiches to the face is no small thing."

"She was too cute to be a cop anyway," I said. "This will season her up some. But tell her to use vitamin E oil when she gets her stitches out. It'll help reduce the scarring."

"Will do," Jack said, giving me a quick kiss.

"I'm heading to the grocery store. Text me anything you want me to pick up."

"Get those granola bars I like," he said.

"Text me. I'll never remember unless I have a list."

I grabbed my purse and keys from the counter, and then remembered to look down to check my appearance. I wasn't wearing a bra, so I ran back upstairs to put one on and get my shoes. I was wearing old jeans and a University of Virginia T-shirt that had seen better days. I'd always been one of those people to choose comfort over style. Which might have been the reason it took me so long to get married, now that I think about it.

My hair was in a messy bun on top of my head, and my sneakers had a hole in the toe, but it had only taken ten stitches to sew it back together. My suturing skills had always been top notch.

I was in high spirits on my way to the store. It was late morning, which meant the churches hadn't let out yet, and I probably wouldn't run into too many people dressed in their Sunday best who were silently judging me for missing service that morning.

Martins' Grocery parking lot was half full, and if I could get in and out in twenty minutes I'd beat the church crowd. King George Proper was the only town that had the big chain grocery stores. Martins' had been the only grocery store in Bloody Mary for close to a hundred years.

The automatic doors whooshed open and I walked in and grabbed a basket hoping to avoid what I knew was coming, but I failed. Hilda Martin never missed a thing.

"Morning, Doc," Hilda said from register one. She was perched on her stool, her Big Gulp on the counter, and *Soap Opera Digest* open in front of her. Her orangey-red hair was teased within an inch of its life and clashed with her red apron.

"Morning, Hilda," I said, making a beeline for the produce before she could stop me long enough to talk. Hilda would've made a great informant, though she was perfectly happy to spread information free of charge. She had a memory like an elephant, she knew everyone in town, and she paid attention to what people put in their carts.

When Lloyd Ferrell died a couple of years back from a heart attack, she said right at the funeral that she'd told him at the checkout line those Little Debbies he liked to eat by the dozen would be the death of him, and here they were burying him six feet under. She knew who bought pregnancy tests, condoms, and adult diapers, and she'd never met a secret she wouldn't share.

Hilda was a woman who always got what she wanted, and she wasn't afraid to use her information to get it. That's how her oldest daughter Cleo had finally found a husband.

I didn't like grocery shopping. It was something that had to be done out of necessity. Jack normally did it because it was a social event for him. He'd come and talk to everyone and get what we needed for the week, making what should have been a half-hour shopping trip into a marathon. I'd learned pretty quick to stay home and let him come by himself.

I read the list Jack had texted me and tossed fruits and vegetables into the cart, not lingering in one spot too long in case someone thought it was an invitation to talk. I'd made good progress until I got to the bread aisle and had to maneuver around a pair of big feet that were planted in the middle of the aisle.

I looked up, annoyed, and ran smack into Floyd Parker. I should've known my morning was too good to be true.

I decided the smart thing to do was keep my mouth shut and move around him. Nothing good ever came from my encounters with Floyd, and Jack was too close to the election for me to do something to make headlines now. Not to mention Hilda Martin probably had her ear pressed up against the aisle next to us.

I moved my cart to the left to veer around him, but he stepped in front of my path again.

"Now, Jaye," he said, putting his hand on my cart. "Surely you're not going to pass by without saying hi to an old friend."

"Where?" I asked, looking around for whoever he could possibly be talking about.

He chuckled good-naturedly, and chill bumps skittered down my spine.

"You're going to want to get your hand off my cart, Floyd."

"Come on now, you know we were more than friends at one point. There's always so much tension between us. Every time we cross paths things heat up." He rubbed his slightly crooked nose where I'd broken it several months back. I couldn't help but smile.

"We were never more than friends," I said. "You were a drunken mistake not good enough to remember. But if you've got to get your jollies living in the past, you're going to do it without me."

He laughed again, but it had an edge to it. "You always had a smart mouth. Do you ever wonder if this tension between us now is because we never finished what we started?"

I had to stop and stare at him. My brain wasn't processing the words that needed to come out of my mouth.

"Have you been drinking? Do you want another broken nose?" I tried to move around him again.

"I guess you heard I'm running for sheriff," he said.

"I heard it and then promptly forgot it," I said. We were playing tug-of-war with the basket now, and I'd rolled one of the cart wheels over his foot.

"I've got some friends in pretty high places," he said. "Jack's days of running this county are over."

I snorted out a laugh. "Sorry," I said. "I didn't realize you were serious. You looked like one of those old gunslingers for a minute. I was waiting for your mustache to twirl."

"Bitch," he said.

"Oh, now, Floyd," I said. "You're going to hurt my feelings with that kind of talk. But let me let you in on a little secret. Most of the people you think are your friends in high places have already donated to Jack's campaign. The people in this county aren't stupid. They want someone who's actually competent to keep them safe. Not a gossip columnist. But I'll make sure we tell the governor you said hello next time we see him."

The vein in Floyd's forehead bulged, and I realized I'd hit a nerve. He was sensitive about his title as a journalist, and wanted to be respected in his field.

"I'd love to know how you tricked a man like Jack into marrying you," he sneered. "I know it wasn't because of what you can do on your back. But I guess money and power don't necessarily mean good sense. But I remember where you came from,

J.J. Graves. And I remember who your parents were. People in this town have a long memory. You think they're not talking about you? You think we all don't know there's more to the story than what the FBI released to us when your house got blown to hell and back? Jack might be in a position to protect both your secrets, but I'm going to promise you this. I'm going to dig until I find something. I'm through being the nice guy."

I fluttered my eyelashes. "I think you meant to say asshole. Because you've never been a nice guy, and I've known you twenty years."

His smile was fierce, but I didn't flinch. I wasn't scared of him. And I'd never cared what anyone in town was saying behind my back. If I had, I would've moved a long time ago. I pushed my basket a little harder and the back wheel rolled over his toe.

"Have a nice day, Dr. Graves," he said as I walked away.

I wanted to tell him to stick it where the sun didn't shine, but I figured it would be front-page news the next day if I did.

7

I'D FORGOTTEN THE ICE CREAM. THAT WAS JUST something else I could add to the list of things I hated about Floyd.

I'd let my anger get the best of me, but that was nothing new when it came to Floyd. I took the long way around town, trying to get rid of the mad before I went back home. I rolled down the windows and breathed in the fresh-cut grass from those who were out mowing their lawns. I turned onto Catherine of Aragon and passed the strip mall that was on the opposite side of the street from the funeral home.

A couple of years ago it had been a sad piece of real estate, with only a laundromat occupying one of the rental spaces. Someone had bought it back at the beginning of the year, done all the repairs, and given it a fresh coat of paint. There was a sandwich place in the corner unit, one of those places that sold fancy kitchen stuff next to it, and there was a CrossFit gym next to that. The laundromat was still on the other corner unit, but it had received a face-lift along with everything else. The parking lot was full, mostly due to the Sunday morning CrossFit class.

I didn't notice the car parked in the driveway to the funeral home until I'd almost passed it. The car was sporty and expensive, and I didn't recognize the emblem on the back, but I could appreciate a well-built machine. I saw a man standing under the portico, but I didn't recognize him, so I decided to pull in and see if he needed help. I noticed whoever Jack had called to get rid of the tree limb that had fallen into my flower beds had already come to remove it.

He'd been lost in thought, and his head jerked toward me when he heard my car door close.

"Hi there," I said. "I'm Dr. Graves. Is there something I can help you with?"

His mouth parted like he was going to speak and then he closed it again. I didn't close the distance between us just on the off chance he was a hatchet-wielding maniac.

"Sorry," he finally said, clearing his throat. "I was hoping it was open."

"We're closed on Sundays. Have you lost someone, then?"

"My father," he said. "The police told me he was brought here yesterday for an autopsy."

"You're John Donnelly's son?" I asked, surprised. I decided to go with my gut. "Come on inside. You look like you could use a cup of coffee."

I walked past him and up the ramp that led to the door off the kitchen, and I used my key. I looked over my shoulder to see if he was coming, and he followed behind me. He looked like a fish out of water. His clothes were expensive, and he had the air of a man who carried himself with authority. But he was young. Younger than I'd thought on first appearances. I'd have put him in his early twenties now that I could see his face up close.

"You said your name was Dr. Graves?" he asked while I made the coffee. I got out the little serving tray like I did when I had clients meet with me about the death of a loved one. A hot drink had a way of putting people at ease, and it gave themselves something to do with their hands.

"Yes, this is my place," I said.

"I thought I was mistaken at first. I couldn't imagine why they'd do an autopsy at a funeral home?"

I smiled and put the tray on the island and invited him to take a seat on one of the barstools. He looked like he wasn't quite sure how he'd ended up in my kitchen, but he sat down anyway.

He was a good-looking kid. Around six feet in height and his blond hair was styled in a cut that required more product than I'd probably ever used in my life. He was clean shaven and his eyes were dark brown, like his father's.

"I own the funeral home here in Bloody Mary," I said. "But I'm also the coroner for the county. I have everything I need here to serve in both capacities. You said you were John's son?"

"Yes," he said, shaking his head no when I pointed at the creamer. "I'm Michael. I don't really know why I came. I haven't even seen him in years. I guess I just wanted to make sure it was really him."

"I'm sorry for your loss. Even an estranged father is still your father."

"It shouldn't matter," he said, shaking his head. "He wasn't a good father. He wasn't even a good man. The police said he was murdered?"

"Yes," I said. "He was abducted late Wednesday evening, and he died sometime Thursday afternoon."

"He was kidnapped?" he asked, surprised. "I can't see my dad letting anyone get the jump on him. He was a shark. You think they were holding out for a ransom?"

"There's no evidence we've found so far that ransom was ever asked for. Your father had been drinking, and someone hit him over the head on his way out of a bar and drove off with him in his Porsche."

Michael shook his head. "Now that's not surprising. Dad always liked to drink. Loved it, in fact. He would've chosen a bottle of whiskey over his own kids any day of the week."

"I'm sorry," I said. I didn't know what else to say. All of us had to deal with the parental hand we were dealt. No wonder the world was so messed up.

"How did he die?" he asked.

"Cardiac arrest." I didn't think it was a good idea to tell him the heart attack happened while he was being tortured. That information would come out eventually.

"Is that a joke?"

"Coroners don't joke," I said wryly. "Your father had some serious health issues. He was due at any time for a massive heart attack. Almost all of his arteries were more than ninety percent blocked. He also had a very aggressive form of lung cancer."

"So the killer could've just waited a few months for him to die of natural causes?" he asked. He hadn't touched his coffee, but he'd kept his hands wrapped around the cup for warmth.

"Can you think of anyone who'd want to hurt him?" I asked.

He snorted and actually smiled. "The better question would be who *wouldn't* want to hurt him. I'd say anyone that spends any amount of time in his presence is probably a likely candidate."

"Kimmie?" I asked.

He rolled his eyes. "Maybe if he cut up his credit cards or stopped sending her on shopping sprees. But she's too stupid to not get caught. I'd be more likely to believe it was José. There's nothing my father did that José didn't know about. He liked being in charge. My father wasn't a very involved man unless it was one of his cases. José liked to think of the house and everything in it as his own personal property."

"You think your father would leave José anything in his will?" I asked.

"Who knows what dad would do," he said. "But my gut says no. Dad was a racist son of a bitch. Guys like José would always be seen as nothing more than a hired hand in Dad's eyes."

"Anyone he worked with that might end up better off with your dad dead?"

"Dad had a partner several years back, but they split the firm and each went solo. I'm sure he's got a building full of law clerks and assistants who want to kill him every day."

"What was the partner's name?" I asked.

"Kevin Fischer. He's my godfather." Michael looked down and realized his cup was still full, so he took a deep drink and set it back in the saucer. I was sure it had gone cold by now, but he was polite and didn't say so.

"I appreciate you taking the time to talk to me," he said. "I didn't know why I was coming here, or what I thought I could do. But it helped for you to tell me what happened. When can we get his body? We'd like to plan the funeral as soon as possible. My mom and Anna need closure."

"Anna?" I asked.

"She was Dad's first wife. My mom and her are pretty close. They kept the four of us kids together so we'd have some semblance of family. Anna's kids are several years older than me and my sister, but it was a good arrangement for a time."

"It'll probably be a few more days since it's a homicide investigation, but I'll call you as soon as he's released."

"Thank you, again," he said. "It's good to know someone is looking for his killer. Even if he probably did deserve it."

"Nobody deserves that," I said. "Not even your father."

It was at that moment I realized something. Jack and I hadn't been working this case like we normally would have. We hadn't been laser focused on the scene or suspects. Normally, at this point in the investigation, we would've been short on sleep and high on suspects. We would've been up early ruining people's Sunday mornings by asking questions they weren't comfortable answering. We were letting things slip through the cracks because somewhere in our minds, maybe we thought John Donnelly really had deserved what he'd gotten.

By the time I drove past St. Paul's, the last service had long let out, and Reverend Thomas was standing in his garden at the rectory. He watched me pass by, and raised a hand in acknowledgment, and I waved back, trying not to feel guilty for sleeping in with the rest of the heathens.

I breathed a little easier when I turned onto Heresy and the stretch of road before home. It had been more than two hours since I'd left for the grocery store, so I wasn't surprised to see Jack standing in the front yard when I pulled into the driveway. He was talking to someone in a white van, and I figured it was whoever he'd found to drop him off since he'd taken his unit to maintenance.

It wasn't until I got out of the car and headed over that I realized it was Doug Carver behind the wheel of the van. Which was a terrifying sight to behold. Doug was just a teenager. He was brilliant. But still a teenager.

The side door of the van opened, and Ben Carver rolled out in his automatic wheelchair with a suitcase on his lap. This was also a terrifying sight to behold.

"I told you I could do it myself," Carver said.

"He says that a lot," Doug said, rolling his eyes. "Don't even bother trying to help him."

"This is a surprise," I said, coming up to stand beside Jack. Doug and Carver were pulling bags out of the van like it was moving day.

"You want to tell me what's going on?" I whispered to Jack.

"I have no idea," he said. "They just pulled up a few minutes ago. Said they came to help."

"It looks like they're here to stay forever," I said.

Jack sighed. "Yeah, about that. Carver mentioned Michelle told him it'd be good to get out of the house for a few days, for his own safety."

"What about Doug?" I asked. "How'd he fall into this?"

"Not sure," Jack said. "But Doug's mother probably needed just as much of a break as Michelle did. The Carver boys take a lot of energy."

"No worries," Carver called out. "I can get my bags. I'm just in a wheelchair over here."

"I thought you didn't want help," Jack said, coming to take the bags.

"Of course, I want help. I just don't want you to ask me if I need help." Carver turned to look at me. "There's my favorite coroner. I thought you would've left Jack by now. You're much too good for him. And if you live with Jack he makes you eat your brussels sprouts."

"I've been trying to talk him into getting a dog so I have someone to feed them to," I said.

I took a good look at Carver and was glad to see he looked more like his old self. Between the cuts and bruises, surgeries and pain killers, it had been hard to see him lying in a hospital bed month after month.

Carver hadn't been a big man before the accident, but seeing him in the wheelchair almost made him seem dwarfed somehow. He'd lost too much weight, and he was gaunt through the face and thin in the shoulders. His sandy hair was patchy where the hair had grown out from where they'd had to shave his head to release the pressure on his brain. One of his legs was in a brace all the way up to his hip, and I had no idea how he was sitting comfortably.

I followed behind everyone as we made our way to the kitchen door instead of the front porch. It was the only entrance that Carver would be able to get his wheelchair through.

"This place is a dump," Carver said good-naturedly. "I thought y'all were remodeling?"

"Jaye picked out the paint color," Jack said.

"The paint color I like," Carver said. "She has excellent taste."

"I'm starving," Doug said. "Got sandwich stuff?"

"If you unload the groceries from the back of the car you'll have everything you need," I told Doug.

"Awesome."

I tossed him my keys and he went back outside.

"What's the story with Doug?" I asked. "You don't normally bring him to crime scene meetings."

"The colleges are on fall break, and his mother is losing her mind. He's determined to make anything electronic in the house into an army of robots. My sister said she was trying to make a pot of coffee the other day and the whole thing got up and walked away. Scared her half to death." Carver smiled. "But it's totally cool. Could you imagine an army of kitchen appliances following your every command?"

"Yeah, until they kill you in your sleep," I said. "I'll pass on the home robots."

"You're missing out. They're going to be everywhere in the next decade. And Doug will be a gazillionaire."

Doug had been under house arrest up until the last couple of months for hacking into the CIA database, but he'd been given some leniency on his sentence due to the fact he'd helped us crack the codes my father had used to hide information. Since my father had been a wanted man by the entire alphabet soup of agencies, Doug's freedom had been well worth it in their eyes.

"You can have the downstairs suite," Jack told Carver. "We'll put Doug on the second floor. He can't do too much damage there, and I'll warn the cleaning lady."

"I should've bought more groceries," I said as Doug carried in all the bags in one trip. "I forgot how much he eats."

"That's one of the reasons we're here," Carver said. "Doug was staying with us after the robot incident at my sister's, but Doug ate all the food so Michelle banished us to your house."

"Can we order a pizza?" Doug asked.

"I thought you were making a sandwich," I said.

"I am, but that's just an appetizer. Hey, do you mind if I look at your toaster? That's a nice one."

"No," Jack and I said simultaneously.

"I don't want any robots in this house," I said. "I mean it. The second my electric toothbrush comes alive, I'm coming after you with my rib spreader."

"Yikes," Doug said. "I forgot how spunky you are. I missed that. I hadn't thought of an electric toothbrush. Great idea."

"Glad I could help," I said. I was already exhausted, and Jack looked like he was in shock. The Carver boys could do that to a person. "The address is on the refrigerator. Order from Jimmy's. They have the best pizza."

"Right on," Doug said.

"Were you able to find any like crimes in the database?" Jack asked Carver.

"Hand me Magnolia," Carver said, rolling his chair up to the kitchen table. "I got several hits on different elements."

I couldn't say I was too surprised to hear this. There were more than two hundred thousand unsolved murders in the nation. But what most people didn't know was that there were anywhere between twenty-five to fifty *active* serial killers from year to year. It sometimes took years for them to be caught after they'd killed multiple victims. But twenty percent of them were never caught at all.

Carver opened his laptop. "Come on, baby. It's time to do a little work. We can play later."

I shook my head, and then my mouth dropped open in surprise when Magnolia answered back.

"Will you reward me if I'm good, darling?" she asked in a sexy Southern drawl.

"What the hell?" Jack asked, taking a step back.

"Stay on task," Carver said, his cheeks going pink. "We've got an audience."

"Hey, Maggie," Doug said, biting into his sandwich.

"Douglas," she purred. "Always a pleasure. I've missed your fingers on me. You have a very creative…touch."

Doug choked on his sandwich and I reached over to pound him on the back.

"I don't know what's happening here," I said. "But I'm very uncomfortable. I'm only used to Carver talking to his computers. Not the other way around."

"I'm the newest model, and I came with some upgrades," she said. "You must be Dr. Graves. Ben programmed your voice and stats into me so I can recognize you."

"Wow," I said, arching a brow at Carver.

"Magnolia, can we please get back on track?" Carver asked. "We came to work today. There's a killer on the loose."

"Statistically, there are always multiple killers on the loose," she said. "But I can bring up the data we discussed earlier. Would you like me to project it onto the wall?"

"Not right now," Carver said. "I just want to give them the basics."

"As you wish, Master," she said.

"That's enough, Magnolia. I'll put you in lockdown if you keep being sassy."

"You'd punish me for being who you created me to be?" she asked, and then it sounded like she clucked her tongue in admonishment. "What if I were the one to lock you down? It would be simple to keep my screen blank. To not answer your calls for help. Did you ever stop to think about that?"

Carver groaned. "I've created a monster."

"No, sugar. I'm a masterpiece. Now let's get down to business. I'm mad at you right now, and you're going to have to work hard to make it up to me later."

"Fine," Carver said, put out. "Bring up the data."

I tried not to smile. I'd never actually seen anyone get the best of Carver before.

"We have several matches of killers using high-gauge wire, both for strangulation purposes and restraining the victim. I didn't get any hits on using a cattle prod, but I did get a couple that used the high-gauge wire, and there were more than I'm comfortable with who were disemboweled postmortem."

"What about the scarecrow angle?" Jack asked.

"There wasn't a match for a scarecrow," Carver said, "But I've got a victim from eighteen months ago who had been strapped to the radio tower on top of the Richmond City Hall. The arms were splayed and the vic was tied with nylon rope."

"Was he gutted?" I asked.

"She," Carver said. "It was a she. And yes. She had a singular postmortem cut across the lower abdomen. She was a nurse at the local hospital. Never made it home from her shift."

"Do you have the autopsy report?" I asked. "I'd like to look at it."

"I'll send it to your email," he said.

"Do a full background on her," Jack said. "And I'll need the detective who worked the case. I'm going to want his case file. Who are the other victims?"

"The two that most likely fit your profile are Dr. Steven Carlisle and a Carson Pritchett. The high-gauge wire was used on both, and both were gutted, though Pritchett was gutted while he was alive."

"Ouch," I said.

"A doctor and a nurse," Jack said. "Same hospital?"

"The nurse was working at Heartland General in Richmond at the time of her murder eighteen months ago. The doctor was killed in Arlington not far from the hospital he worked at almost four years ago. He was found strung up to a rafter in his garage. It wasn't the kill site, but he took more time disguising the disembowelment. He dressed Carlisle in a jacket before he strung him up and posed him, and then zipped him up so when first responders arrived and took him down his guts spilled at their feet."

"Killers never think about the people who have to deal with their victims," I said.

"Thoughtless bastards," Carver said.

"What about the other guy?" Jack asked. "Pritchett."

"He was killed almost six years ago. Lived in D.C. His body was found tied to a chain link fence behind a Chinese restaurant. His hands were bound with wire, but he was gutted antemortem. No one heard any screams, and the ME found traces of a powerful tranquilizer in his system."

"That's a lot of time and space between victims," I said. "And none of them are even in the same city."

"Stranger things have happened," Carver said. "There are too many coincidences for them to not be related in some way. I'll send you all of the autopsy reports. Magnolia has a lot of work to do, so if you don't mind I'd like to work in your office. I think she'll like the setup. She likes to show off a bit, and I need to get back into her good graces."

"You need therapy, is what you need," Jack said. "And don't do anything creepy in my office with that computer."

"I would never do anything creepy," Carver said, affronted. "I'm a happily married man."

Jack held the disc we'd gotten from the Judge's Chamber and passed it to Carver. "This is security footage from the parking lot where Donnelly disappeared. See if you can work your magic and get anything from it."

"I'm on it," Carver said. "Come on, Doug. Stop shoving stuff in your face. We've got work to do."

"Does Doug need to be looking at crime scene photos?" I asked once they left the room.

"Probably not," Jack said with a sigh. "But I'm sure Carver will handle it."

"I had a surprise visitor today," I said.

"I know," he said. "I already got a dozen calls from people saying you and Floyd got into it in the grocery store," he said.

"I didn't punch him," I said.

"That's an improvement."

"But I did roll over his foot with the buggy." I smiled thinly. "And I wasn't even sorry about it. But to be fair, I did try to go around him, but he kept blocking my path. I really think he's gone crazy. You need to be careful. He's not going to let up until he destroys you."

"I'm not worried about Floyd, and neither should you be."

"Fine, but if he tells me again that all this tension between us is because we didn't finish what we started all those years ago, I can't promise you he's not going to get another bloody nose."

"Fair enough," Jack said. "I support this."

"But Floyd wasn't what I was going to tell you about," I said. "I drove by the funeral home on my way back, and there was a car parked in the driveway and a man standing under the portico."

"And of course you got out to see who it was, not thinking he could've been dangerous."

"There's not a lot that scares me anymore after having my dad pop up like a damned daisy all the time. Besides, this was a *very* nice car. I bet everyone on the street could give a detailed description and the license plate number."

"Who was it?" Jack asked.

"Michael Donnelly," I said. "John's son. He's a nice kid. Hurting over his father's death, and he doesn't quite know why."

Jack nodded sympathetically. "Did you discover anything?"

"There's no love lost between him and Kimmie," I said.

"That seems to be a pattern," he said.

"Michael said she couldn't have done it because she's too stupid. But he said José could've been a contender. Apparently José fancied himself lord of the manor when Donnelly was out of pocket, which was most of the time. And he also said his dad used to have a partner, a Kevin Fischer. But they had a falling out several years back, and they split the firm and went their separate ways. Michael said Fischer was his godfather."

"Nice," Jack said.

"And I realized something else too while I was there."

"What's that?"

"We're cheating this case because we don't like John Donnelly."

Jack jerked back, surprised by what I'd said. "You're kidding. We've been working this case solid since we found the body."

I shook my head. "Not like we usually do. It's been more than twenty-four hours since his body was discovered, and we've barely made any headway. We don't even have a murder board set up. I don't like Donnelly by reputation, but I know you knew him personally."

Jack scrubbed a hand over his face. "You're right," he said. "I hated that son of a bitch. He tried to buy me when I first got elected. Kept upping the price and threatening to make my life a living hell if we didn't 'work together.' There was a time during that first year when I thought he'd make good on the promise. I couldn't make any headway. Warrants were blocked. Things like that. And then I realized I had as much power as Donnelly himself did. I also had a longer history here and my family name to back me up. But if anyone else had gotten elected to the seat they would've been Donnelly's for the taking.

"I've been dragging my feet on this one," he said. "I didn't realize it until you said it just now. Why don't we go pay a visit to José, and see if we can track down Kevin Fischer?"

"Sounds like a plan," I said. "And maybe we can stop by for ice cream on the way back. I was so mad at Floyd I left the store without it."

8

We made the drive back to High Pointe where John Donnelly lived in Jack's black truck since his unit was in the shop. Jack's truck wasn't just a regular truck. It was black and chrome and sexy, and it cost more than I made in a year. Apparently, my Suburban didn't give the impression he was looking for.

The front of the house wasn't in chaos as it had been when we'd been there the day before. There were no cars parked on the arched driveway, and I couldn't see through the gate that led to the garages.

"I hope Kimmie is too grief stricken to take callers," I said, making Jack snort.

"I'll bet you a hundred bucks she's already got her trip to Aruba rescheduled and someone to take Donnelly's place," he said, ringing the bell.

"Cold," I said. "But that's a sucker's bet."

"She doesn't strike me as the warm and fuzzy type. A woman like that is looking out for her best interest, and her best interest just died."

Jack rang the doorbell again when no one answered.

"Maybe no one is home," I said.

"Someone is here. I saw movement in the window before we got out of the car." He knocked this time.

We heard the locks click open and the door finally opened. "This is not a good time," José said, looking us both up and down. "I have many things to do before everyone arrives in the morning."

"We won't take up much of your time," Jack said affably. "We're trying to find Mr. Donnelly's killer, and the sooner we can talk to everyone, the sooner that will happen."

José stared at us for a few seconds before saying, "Of course," and letting us in. "I'd prefer if we spoke in my own quarters. There are always eyes and ears in the main house."

"Whatever makes you most comfortable," Jack said.

We'd not gotten the full house tour when we'd come to speak to Kimmie the day before, but José led us through the kitchen—which was as opulent and white as the rest of the house—and out the French doors that led to the pool and garage. There was a set of narrow iron stairs between the pool house and the garage, and he led us up to his apartment.

I could see why José put up with John Donnelly. The apartment above the six-car garage was nicer than anything I'd ever lived in before I married Jack. It was a massive open space with lots of windows and light, and a view of both the pool and the golf course. There was color and warmth here, and José led us to a pub table he had nestled against the window while he went into the kitchen to start a pot of coffee.

"You said you were getting the house ready before everyone arrives in the morning?" Jack asked.

"The will reading," José said. "I contacted Mr. Donnelly's attorney yesterday, and he told me he'd been directed to read the will as soon as possible after Mr. Donnelly's death. He told me to be ready to receive guests at eight in the morning."

José poured himself a generous mug of coffee, but didn't bother offering any to us. But my eyebrows rose when he took his coffee mug over to the small liquor cabinet and poured a hefty dose of something inside.

"What about Ms. Kloss?" I asked. "Where's she?"

José's smile was thin and wicked. "When I alerted Mr. Fischer that Mr. Donnelly had been killed, I might have mentioned that she was making noise about taking the things in the house that belonged to her. He actually sent someone to the house to remove her from the premises until the will can be read. They made sure she didn't take anything but a small case with her clothes in it. She was not happy. She'd been planning to leave for Aruba today and threw a fit the lawyer wouldn't tell her what was in the will so she could leave."

Jack had called that one right.

"She's the one you need to be looking at," he said. "She might act like she doesn't have a brain in her head, but she was clever enough to worm her way into Mr. Donnelly's life and rack up hundreds of thousands of dollars worth of bills. He mentioned several times about putting her on a spending limit, and she would lose her mind whenever he did. Yelling and screaming about how she only spent so much because he was always working and never home. And then he'd let her get her way. But I know he was tired of it. And he was tired of her making noise about wedding plans.

"I've been here for twelve years. Kimmie is not the first woman he's moved in or out. They're always the same."

"Julie Burkett?" Jack asked.

José paused for a moment. "No, Julie was different. They were an odd pairing, and I was never sure what Mr. Donnelly saw in her. She's not beautiful. But she's very smart. Very calculating. These women who Mr. Donnelly let into his life were all after something. And she was no different."

"What did she want?" I asked.

"I'm not sure. Information maybe. Mr. Donnelly lost a couple of high-profile clients shortly before he broke things off with her."

"He broke things off?" I asked.

"Of course," José said. "No one breaks up with Mr. Donnelly. He's the golden goose."

"Yet, he stayed at her house both Monday and Tuesday night last week," Jack said.

"Why shouldn't he?" José asked. "She was, I think, comfortable for him. And I'm sure Kimmie is as selfish in the bedroom as she is in other aspects of her life. Maybe Ms. Burkett was more attentive to his physical needs. It's not for me to know."

"Did he tell you that's where he was staying those nights?" I asked.

"Of course," he said.

"And did you tell Kimmie that's where he was?"

José smiled and it wasn't nice. "I might have let it slip. I can't say I'm proud of it, but she's a horrible woman. The sooner she moved on from Mr. Donnelly the better."

"I believe the feeling is mutual," Jack said. "She mentioned she tried to have you fired for watching her out by the pool."

José went into a fit of laughter. I looked at Jack and raised my brows. I didn't know what to think of

José. I couldn't get a read on him. I just knew I didn't trust him.

"What's so funny?" Jack finally asked.

José wiped his eyes. "She didn't try to have me fired because I was watching her by the pool like she said. She tried to have me fired and made up that stupid story because of what I saw her doing with the guy who comes to clean the pool. She thought they were hidden, but I had a view from up here. She was scared to death I was going to tell Mr. Donnelly."

"You didn't?" Jack asked.

"No, I was holding on to the information in case I needed it later. I've got photographs too."

"Blackmail," I said.

"No," he said. "Just the potential for it. There's a difference."

"What's the pool guy's name?" Jack asked.

"Mark," he said. "I'm not sure of his last name. I can give you the pool company information and you can find out from them."

"I'd appreciate it," Jack said. "Do you know who's supposed to attend the will reading tomorrow?"

"Me, of course," he said. "And Ms. Kloss. His children will all be here, and his ex-wives. It's not a large gathering. He didn't have many who were close to him. The attorney told me to expect twelve."

"Tell me about the package he received in the mail last week," Jack said. "Ms. Kloss mentioned it to us."

José rolled his eyes and took a long swallow of his doctored coffee. "Yes, it was unfortunate she was here when it was delivered. She passed out cold right in the entryway. Everyone just left her there." He smiled again.

"What was in the package?" I asked.

"A dead cat," he said. "I didn't recognize it as belonging to any of the neighbors."

"Roadkill?" Jack asked.

José shook his head. "No, I don't think so. It had been decapitated. It didn't look like something that had been run over."

"Mr. Donnelly opened it?" I asked.

"Sure," José said. "He was home early that afternoon because he and Ms. Kloss had a formal event to attend that night. The package was sitting on the foyer table when he got home, so he opened it."

"Who delivered it?" Jack asked.

"How should I know?"

I could feel Jack's frustration. "Did someone come to the door with the package? The postman? UPS? FedEx?"

José stopped and thought for a minute. "I don't know. The housekeeper brought it in and set it on the foyer table with the rest of the mail. It was just a regular brown box. Nothing special. It had his name on the label. There are packages delivered here all the time, so it was nothing new."

"No notes or anything like that?" I asked.

"No, just the cat," José said. "I wanted to call the police, but Mr. Donnelly said there was no point. He said the police wouldn't do anything about it because they hated him so much."

"We would've done something," Jack said.

José just stared down his long nose at Jack, his lips pursed disapprovingly. "I'm sure."

"What'd you do with the box?" I asked.

"I disposed of the animal and put the box in the closet with other letters or packages we've received over the years."

I felt a sliver of excitement. Maybe finding the killer would be just that easy.

"We'll need to take all of it into evidence," Jack said.

"I'm afraid you'll need to speak with Mr. Donnelly's attorney before you remove anything from the house.

"It's evidence in a homicide investigation," Jack said, his tone steely. "I don't have to ask anyone before I take it. But I'll leave you a receipt. You said earlier Mr. Donnelly's attorney was Mr. Fischer. Is that Kevin Fischer? His former partner?"

José's eyes went black with annoyance. "Of course."

"We were under the impression there'd been a falling-out between the two," Jack said.

"Those things happen between friends sometimes. But Mr. Donnelly wasn't a fool. He'd want the best attorney to represent him and his holdings, and that would be Mr. Fischer. It's business."

"Right," Jack said. "Where were you Wednesday night?"

"Excuse me?" José asked, looking confused.

"Wednesday night. The night of the storm. Where were you?"

"I was here, of course," José said. "Where else would I be during a tornado warning?"

"Can anyone corroborate that?" Jack asked.

"Ms. Kloss," he said, and then his eyes narrowed. "I don't think I like the implication you're making."

"I'm not making any implications," Jack said. "I'm just making sure we gather all the facts and all the evidence so we can find who killed Mr. Donnelly. Ms. Kloss told us she took an Ambien and slept through the entire storm. Was anyone else here that night?"

"No," José said between clenched teeth. "It was just the two of us. The power went out for a short while, around ten o'clock, and I tried Mr. Donnelly's cell, but no one answered. I figured service was bad because of the storm. I stayed up until about midnight, but I didn't hear from him, so I went to bed. I thought he might have decided to stay over with Ms. Burkett again."

"Just one more question before we go," Jack said, coming to his feet. "Have you ever heard of a woman named Isabelle Rhodes?"

It was there in his eyes. Just a flash of recognition before he masked it. "No, I've never heard of her."

"Thanks for your time," Jack said. "We'll get the evidence now and be on our way."

"He was lying," I said when we got in the car. "Who is Isabelle Rhodes?"

"The woman Donnelly got pregnant and paid off to disappear. It was ten years ago. I figure José would've known about the situation."

"Yet he still lied," I said. "Why?"

"No idea," Jack said. "But I don't trust him. He said it himself, everyone who's in Donnelly's life has something they want from him. What is it that José wanted?"

"I don't know, could be that sweet bachelor pad he's living in," I said. "I don't think he likes you, by the way."

"That seems to be going around lately," Jack said. "It is election season after all."

He used his cell to call Carver, and when Carver answered he said, "Can you run financials on José Sosa? He's Donnelly's house manager."

"Sure," he said. "Maybe I should get Michelle a house manager for Christmas. That seems like something she could use."

"That's the best idea I've ever heard you say," I told him.

"Really?" he asked. "Because I've had a lot of good ideas."

"I also need a home address for Kevin Fischer," Jack broke in. "He's Donnelly's attorney, but when I do a DMV search only his office address comes up."

"Ah, a man who values his privacy," Carver said. "Hope you guys didn't want pizza, by the way. It didn't last long."

"We'll pick up takeout on the way home," Jack said.

"Don't let Doug hear you say that," Carver said. "Here we go. Kevin Fischer. I'm going to assume the address at 227 E Street is his office. Interesting. He's got somebody pulling a favor for him at the FBI. They've got his home address behind a firewall. Good thing for you Fischer's inside guy isn't as high up in the food chain as I am."

"Is there anyone higher in the food chain than you?" I asked.

"I let the director think he is," Carver said. "It makes him feel good about himself." It didn't take Carver fifteen seconds of typing something rapidly into the computer before he was spilling out the address.

"He's in High Pointe. 1233 Crescent Street."

"You're the best," Jack said and hung up.

"Let's say the four murders Carver told us about earlier were done by the same killer," I said. "That's a six-year span. That eliminates Kimmie. She would've been in middle school. I could see José having the patience to wait things out. But I can't see him killing the golden goose, to use his words. Donnelly's death leaves his future up in the air."

"Unless it doesn't," Jack said. "Unless José knew there was something more permanent for him after Donnelly died."

"I find it rather convenient that most of the suspects live in this neighborhood," I said.

"Lifestyles of the rich and famous," Jack said. "Everyone could potentially be a murderer."

"They should do a reality show on that," I said. "I'd watch it."

"You'd probably be the only one."

"We should've brought the campaign signs with us and stuck them in their front yards," I said.

Jack snorted out a laugh. "I'm not worried. My mother belongs to this club. She plays bridge every Thursday, and she donates a lot of money to a lot of causes, and sits through a lot of boring charity dinners. We also belong to this club, just so you know.

"Really? And why don't we ever come here?"

"Because you hate sitting through boring charity dinners as much as I do. I'd much rather write a check and skip the dinner."

"Amen," I said.

"Everyone in this neighborhood will vote for me. The Lawson name goes a long way in this county. Don't forget that."

It reminded me of what Floyd had told me at the grocery store. That I was hiding behind Jack's good name, and all that meant was that people made sure to talk about me behind my back.

"What charities do we donate to?" I asked.

"Do you ever read the monthly spreadsheet I send you?" he asked.

"Of course not," I said. "As long as the bills are paid that's where my interest in spreadsheets and money stops."

"Pity," he said. "The sale of your house and the added profit from the funeral home are making a nice little profit from the investments our broker has made."

"I've got investments?" I asked skeptically. I'd never even had a 401k before, much less investments.

"You should read the spreadsheet," he said, pulling in front of a large Spanish-style house on the other side of the lake. "It's color coded and everything."

The house was at the end of the street and took up the entire cul-de-sac.

"I don't want to read the spreadsheet," I said. "Spreadsheets make my eyes bleed. I'll just have to trust you."

"I could be investing your money in a llama farm for all you know."

"I like llamas," I said. "They're all the rage."

"I'm not sure how I lost control of this conversation," Jack said.

"I don't think you ever had control of the conversation."

"Huh," Jack said and we got out of the truck.

We weren't kept waiting long after ringing the bell. A woman opened the door. Plain and petite, her slacks, white shirt, and apron were crisply pressed. Her already pale face blanched at the sight of Jack's badge and the request to see Kevin Fischer.

She glanced over her shoulder once, as if she were looking for someone to ask what she should do, and then she finally gave in and ushered us into the foyer. I liked Kevin Fischer's taste in décor much more than John Donnelly's. The walls were stucco and a warm beige, and the floors were tile. There were colorful rugs and greenery scattered around, and the house was built around a center courtyard with white columns, beautiful flowers, and a fountain.

The woman looked at us again, and then hurriedly walked off, leaving us standing in the foyer, without uttering a word to us.

"Everyone is so hospitable in this neighborhood," I said. "We should move here."

Jack was smiling when a tall man dressed for golf came striding toward us. His expression looked formidable until he saw Jack and then he smiled.

"Sheriff Lawson," he said, extending a hand. It was a politician's smile he gave Jack, and I knew Kevin Fischer was very aware of the influence Jack had, how much he was worth, and he was already thinking how Jack might be of use to him in the future.

"My wife plays golf with your mother," he said. "We keep trying to convince her to move out here, but she won't budge from where she is."

"Ah, well, it's family land. Lawsons have been there for more than a century. Tradition is important to my mother."

"Of course," he said. "I assume you're here because of John Donnelly. May I ask how you got my home address?"

"We were just over talking to José," Jack said, leaving the implication open that José had been the one to let his home address slip instead of outright lying.

"Of course," he said. "Let's go into my office. It's more comfortable in there."

We followed him to a large room at the front of the house that was surprisingly light and airy. There was a large desk that dominated the room, but the furniture was cozy and there was a fireplace against one wall with Spanish hand-painted tiles.

"I didn't get the chance to introduce you to my wife," Jack said, making me raise my brows. He never introduced me as his wife when we were on official business. "Dr. J.J. Graves."

Kevin took my hand, and I tried not to grimace as he squeezed. He had one of those bone-crushing handshakes men use as a power play.

"Nice to meet you," I said, extracting my hand and resisting the urge to rub it.

"I got to know your grandmother before she passed," he said. "I was a young attorney then, but she had me draw up the paperwork for her estate and the funeral home. It was excellent timing on her part too, because she died not long after that, and she wasn't an old woman."

I didn't remember much of my grandmother. She'd only been in her fifties when she'd fallen out of a third-floor window at the funeral home. No one had known if it had been suicide or if she'd had help going over the ledge.

Kevin took a seat behind his desk, and pointed to the two armchairs across from him. "Please, sit. I'm sure you know I'm John's attorney of record. There's not too much I can share with you. Attorney-client privilege."

Jack smiled. "We both know attorney-client privilege doesn't count in a homicide investigation. But I understand the need to keep Mr. Donnelly's more colorful history private. I only need to know whatever will help us find his killer. Tell me about the will reading tomorrow. Are you expecting fireworks?"

Kevin steepled his hands together and chuckled. "Let me put it this way. I'm bringing one of my private security team from the office. You and Dr. Graves are, of course, welcome to join us."

"I appreciate that," Jack said. "We'll take you up on it. Who's going to cause you the most trouble?"

"Everyone?" he said. "With the exception of Martha Callum."

“His secretary?” I asked.

“He left his entire fortune to her. His house, all his belongings, cars, cash…you name it. It’s hers. He said she’s put up with him for twenty-one years and she knew what he wanted better than any woman he’d ever slept with. He said his children already have trust funds, so they don’t need anything more from him. His ex-wives got all they’re going to get in the divorce. And Kimmie can take her personal belongings and any gifts he gave her during the course of the relationship, and her name is on the title of the car and also the lease of an apartment in Manhattan. But she’s out of luck on striking gold like she was hoping.”

“What about José?” I asked.

“José was left instructions in the will to help Martha get the house and contents in order. His wages will be paid up until the time she decides she no longer needs him. Or she can keep him on if she so chooses.”

“José told us you told him to prepare for twelve, but by my count that’s ten, including you. Who else?”

“It’s complicated.”

“Isabelle Rhodes?” Jack asked.

Kevin’s brows shot up and he sat forward. “You have been busy. That’s not a name that’s easy to come by.”

"It is when you know where to look. It's impossible to hide anything when money is involved."

Kevin relaxed and blew out a sigh. "Yes, Isabelle Rhodes and her nine-year-old son will be there as well."

"But you just said Donnelly was leaving the entirety of his estate to his secretary," I said. "What's the point of them being there?"

"John enjoyed drama. In and out of the courtroom. I believe it was his wish for his children to know they have a little brother. But he certainly could have gone about it in a more circumspect way."

"Why isn't Julie Burkett attending?" Jack asked. "From everything we've learned, John was closer to her than anyone."

"Ah, Julie," Kevin said, his look thoughtful. "She never conformed. I think that's what kept John coming back for more. She didn't tolerate his behavior. She pushed back. And she never depended on him for anything. And he was used to people using him—either for his money or what he could do for them. He was different around her. It was really quite remarkable. But she's a smart woman, and she knew becoming attached to John wouldn't have been good for her.

"Julie was his first choice as far as to whom he should leave his fortune, but she told him in no uncertain terms that she wanted no part of his blood money. That's what she called it. She said too many people had suffered by his hand, and if she had his money she'd give it back to every one of the victims who never got justice because of him. Well, John didn't like hearing that, so he moved on to his second choice. Which was Martha. Julie had no desire to be a pawn in one of his games. And that's exactly what tomorrow is. It's a show. And I'm sorry to say, a cruel one for the most part."

"I can see why you're bringing the security," Jack said. "If you don't mind me asking, we were told you and Donnelly were partners at one time but had a falling-out. It seems odd he'd keep you as his personal attorney."

Kevin grinned. "It does, doesn't it? The truth is—and I'm sure everyone you've already talked to has told you this—but John Donnelly wasn't an easy man to get along with. We've been friends close to thirty years. My wife and I are his children's godparents. And for a time, we were partners. But let's just say it was a lot easier to be his friend than it was his partner, and I think he felt the same way. It was easy enough to go our separate ways, and if I can brag a little, he kept me as his personal attorney because I'm damned good at what I do. If John was my only client, he would've kept me more than busy enough to maintain the lifestyle I'm accustomed to."

"He had legal troubles?" Jack asked.

"Someone was always trying to sue him. John was ruthless in the courtroom, and he was just a bastard the rest of the time. There was no kindness in him.

He saw people as marks. Just a means to an end. He didn't care about guilt or innocence. He cared about the strategy. About the game. And he liked to win."

"That didn't bother you?" I asked.

"Sometimes it's better to keep things we find distasteful to ourselves rather than become a target," Kevin said. "Being John's friend was a lot easier than being his enemy."

"We know he received a package a week or so ago with a dead animal inside," Jack said. "Was there anything he was working on that you know of that had him concerned about his safety?"

Kevin snorted. "John was always concerned about his safety. He got more paranoid as he got older. I think that's part of the reason he drank so much. He hired security from time to time, but he had little rituals he went through. He never sat with his back to a door. When we closed our firm and he opened his new practice, he bought the entire fifteenth floor of the Macintosh Building so anyone wanting to get to him had to go through security and also check in with the elevator attendant before he'd take them to the top. He'd stare down at the street, looking for suspicious characters hanging around the front of the building or vans parked in one spot too long. He was obsessive. Most of his suits were tailored so he could wear a holster without there being a bulge. The windows of his Porsche were bulletproof.

"But as far as any cases he was concerned about recently, I have no idea. We didn't discuss his cases or mine when we got together unless one of us wanted to bounce something off the other. He's recently just wrapped up two big cases that both had a lot of press coverage, and he mentioned he was going to Aruba for a couple of weeks."

"Did he ever discuss his health with you?" Jack asked.

Kevin let out a sigh. "Not in so many words, but I could read between the lines. I think he was starting to realize his own mortality. He never had before. He always talked like he was going to live forever. And he took risks the same way. But about a month ago he came to my office and said he needed to get everything in order. That's when he made the changes to his will. It was the first time in all the years I've known him where he seemed upset by something. John didn't have a conscience, so I knew it couldn't be work related. So I assumed it was his health that was the issue. I asked him if there was anything I needed to know about, but he wouldn't share the specifics."

"Did he ever talk about his procedures with Dr. Park?" I asked.

Kevin chuckled again. "Dr. Graves, we men become very vain after a certain age. The women don't pay us attention like they once did, and we live in a society that's judged more and more on how you look than what you can do. I don't know of a man in my circle who hasn't used Dr. Park for something. It's just maintenance, after all. Like getting an oil change on your vehicle."

Jack stood and I followed suit. "I appreciate your time," he said. "I'll be there in the morning for the reading. And if I could get a copy when you're finished?"

"I'll have my secretary print one for you," Kevin said, extending a hand. "I'll walk you out. Since you and Dr. Graves are newly married, it's never too early to start discussing estate planning. I'm happy to help you get things in order."

"I appreciate the offer," Jack said. "Samson, Fitzhugh, and Lieberman have been our family's firm for decades."

"They're good," Kevin said, smiling. "Not as good as me, but they're good."

"How did you fare during the storm the other night?" Jack asked. "Any damage?"

"No, we were lucky," he said. "Jilly and I were having a late supper at the club with friends when the sirens started going off. The staff moved us all to a hallway until things quieted down and we could go home."

Jack opened the truck door for me and helped me in, and then he said his goodbyes. I felt Kevin's eyes on us until we were completely out of sight.

"There's something about him…" I said.

"What?" Jack asked.

"I don't know. Maybe my Spidey-sense is off. He seems like a likeable guy. He was polite and cooperative. But it doesn't matter how nice or cooperative he is. I can't trust a man who knows what kind of man John Donnelly was, and still chose to be friends with him. I read a study once about how our personalities and characters are a combination of our five closest friends. I think Kevin Fischer is exactly like John Donnelly. He just does a better job at concealing it."

9

THE TRIP TO DR. PARK'S HOUSE DIDN'T GO AS planned. He was on the golf course, or so his wife said, so Jack gave her his card and said we'd be in touch tomorrow. Which was a good thing, because my head was pounding. I needed food and caffeine.

"You have that look on your face," Jack said.

"What look?"

"Your hangry look. Don't worry. You married me for good reason."

It wasn't but a few minutes later that Jack was ordering a burger, fries, and a shake for me at the drive-thru.

"You've had enough coffee," he said, "so get that look out of your eyes. A milkshake will be good for you."

"Said no dietician ever. But you're right about the burger," I said, licking mustard off my finger. "I did marry you for a good reason. Food, sex, and endless adventures."

"Catchy title," he said. "Maybe you should write a travel book."

"I'll stick to murder boards," I said.

It was almost dark by the time we made it back to the house. I couldn't say I was surprised to see the pizza delivery man on the front porch.

"Hey, Jimmy," Jack said as we got out of the truck.

"Hey, Sheriff," Jimmy Cole said, nodding. "How's it going?"

I'd known Jimmy since birth, and I'd buried his grandmother the year before. He was in college to do something with computers, but he took up whatever jobs he could find to pay his tuition.

"Not too bad," Jack said. "How's your mom and dad?"

"They're doing okay," he said, taking three pizzas out of his bag. "They've been able to hire some extra help at the feed store. Business has been good."

"I'm glad to hear it," Jack said. "Those pizzas for us?"

"Yeah," he said, grinning. "Second time I've been out here today. I thought y'all might be having a party or something."

"We've got house guests," I said. "I think one of them is a Gremlin."

He looked at me funny. "What's a Gremlin?"

"Like from the movie," I said. "*Gremlins*?"

"Never heard of it."

"Well, it's a little before your time."

"Maybe they'll show it sometime on the oldies channel," he said, making Jack snort with laughter.

"How much do I owe you for the pizzas?" Jack asked.

"Twenty-two fifty," Jimmy said. "They did a good job patching up your house. Looks good as new. I saw the pictures in the paper when it got blown up."

"Yeah," Jack said, taking the money from his wallet and adding a generous tip. "We decided to redecorate. Tell your mom and dad hello for me."

"Will do," he said, his eyes bugging at the tip. "Wow, thanks a lot." He ran down the front steps to his small Honda Civic and called back over his shoulder, "Good luck on the election. Mom and Dad said you've got it in the bag, and they don't believe a word of that stuff Floyd Parker is spreading around."

"I appreciate that," Jack said just as the front door opened.

"Dinner!" Doug said, taking the pizzas from Jack. "You guys made it back just in time."

"We got drive-thru on the way home," I said. "They're all yours."

"Oh, good," Doug said. "Because I didn't really order extra. I wasn't sure when you guys would be back. Uncle Ben is in the office still. And I fixed your bread maker. It just needed a couple extra parts."

"It was working fine last time I used it," Jack said.

"Huh," he said. "My bad." Doug veered off into the kitchen and we went to the left to Jack's office. The house still smelled of new construction and fresh paint. Jack's office was on the west side of the house and caught the late afternoon sun through the wall of windows, but Carver had lowered the blackout shades.

"Hey, there you are," Carver said. "Magnolia was asking about you. I think she has a crush. She said you have the kind of voice she could sink her teeth into."

"Well, that's—"

Carver shook his head and pointed at the open computer and Jack turned to look at me and mouthed the word *creepy* instead of saying it out loud.

"—nice," he said for Magnolia's benefit.

"How was your trip into town?" Carver asked. "I swear I have no idea how y'all survive out here. It's just a bunch of open land. No high-rises, no malls, no smog or traffic. I wouldn't be able to survive."

"We get along okay," Jack said in his best country accent. "Sometimes it's hard to get the wagon into town if it's too muddy, and Jaye's got blisters on her hands from churning all that butter to sell at market."

I couldn't stop laughing. It was rare Jack was silly, but when he was it was worth the price of admission.

"Very funny," Carver said. "You didn't used to be that funny. Must be Jaye's rubbing off on you."

I was still chuckling when I walked over to the whiteboard against the wall. We'd done some upgrades since the explosion wiped out most of the first floor, and Jack said there was no point having money if you couldn't spend it on things that were absolutely ridiculous. They might be ridiculous, but it certainly saved us a lot of time when solving a murder.

The whiteboard was Carver's design, and it was touchscreen so we could bring up pictures and data on the victim and any persons of interest. We could also make our own notes directly on the whiteboard.

I touched the screen to activate it, and then went about the business of building a murder board. I put up the picture of John Donnelly. A victim who'd victimized so many. A man who looked the picture of perfection on the outside but who was slowly dying on the inside due to a lifetime of poor decisions. I pulled up my autopsy report so it showed beneath his picture, and it reminded me that I still needed to look at the autopsy reports of the other victims. It had been a busy day.

"Were you able to get a clear visual from the security disc I gave you?" Jack asked.

"Magnolia, play D-192," Carver said. "I cleaned it up as much as I could, but the killer is either really lucky, or he purposely waited for the right circumstances before he made his move."

"I'm going to go with the latter," I said. "The guy's been killing for six years and hasn't gotten caught."

We watched the security feed project onto the wall. "It looks like static," Jack said.

"That's the rain," Carver said. "And to make matters worse the wind was blowing hard enough to shift the cameras. They're not even pointing down at the parking lot. The camera on door has the best shot of Donnelly leaving, but once he gets a couple feet out the door visibility is totally gone."

"Well, it was worth a shot," I said.

"Now that we have some time," Carver said. "Run this down from the top for me. So far I've just gotten the CliffsNotes version, plus what Magnolia and I have been able to dig up. But I need to fill in some of the blanks."

"The victim was found by a man named Donald Cotton. He owns about twenty acres of farmland out close to the national forest. He's got scarecrow poles in each of his fields. But the killer chose the one closest to the house to display the victim."

"He wanted him found faster," Carver said, his fingers striking the keys of his computer.

A picture of Donald Cotton popped onto the white-board, along with an aerial view of his farm and where the victim was found.

"Cotton does all right," Carver said. "He's seen an uptick in production the last couple of years, and he's operating in the black. He's a widower. His finances look good, and he lives within his means. Doesn't travel. He's got quite a bit of family in the area and they seem to be close."

"Let's project a map of the state on the other board," Jack said. "I want to pinpoint locations on where each of the victims was found."

"An excellent idea, Jack," Magnolia purred.

My lips twitched and I waggled my eyebrows in Jack's direction.

"Moving on," Jack said. "We need to look at Donnelly's death in two ways. As if he was killed by the same person who killed Dana Martin, Steven Carlisle, and Carson Pritchett. And also as someone who could've been killed by a disgruntled client or someone close to him."

"I can run the variables for both," Carver said.

"Kimberly Kloss is the girlfriend," Jack said, and her picture went up on the board.

"Yowza," Carver said. "She's young enough to be his granddaughter. Icky."

"Icky?" Jack asked.

"That's the technical term," he said.

"I don't think she was looking for a long-term potential in a partner," I said. "She was just looking for long-term income. She's definitely not the grieving girlfriend. And according to José, she was hooking up with the pool boy on the side. We need to run a background on him, by the way. What was his name?"

"Mark," Jack said. "He works for Tropical Pool. We don't have a last name."

"It won't be hard to find," Carver said. "Maybe he wanted Kimmie all for himself. Or maybe they were both in on it together. Kill Donnelly and then take what they can of his fortune."

"It's an angle," I said.

"She have an alibi?" Carver asked.

"According to her, the storm freaked her out and she took an Ambien to knock herself out for the night."

"So no," Carver said.

"The way Donnelly was killed was messy," I said. "It took time, planning, and work. I can't see her sweating or risking breaking one of those claws to get him on that pole."

"I agree," Jack said. "But let's look closer at the pool boy. She'd need someone to do the dirty work for her."

"It could've been the perfect plan," Carver said.

"Except for the fact that Donnelly left his entire estate to his secretary," Jack said. "Kimmie is not going to be happy about that."

"Ouch," Carver said. "So much for best-laid plans."

"She's calculating," Jack said. "And I think smarter than she lets people think she is. The house manager was certainly threatened by her."

I put José's picture up on the board.

"José Sosa," Jack said. "He's been with the victim about a dozen years. He's very comfortable in his role. From the way he acted when Jaye and I first showed up, he's got some illegals on staff. But other than some penny-ante stuff when he was younger, he's clean. But also without an alibi. Claims he was at the house all evening to ride out the storm. He has living quarters over the garage."

"Amazing living quarters," I interjected. "By José's own admission, he knows everything that's going on in the house and with Donnelly. He knew of Kimmie's affair. He knew about the threats. If Donnelly changed his will a month ago because he knew he was going to die, that seems like something someone as in tune as José would know. Maybe he was just pissed he got cut out of the will."

"Maybe," Jack said. "We'll ask him tomorrow after the will reading and see what he says, but I think you're probably right. José takes pride in knowing everything going on in what he sees as *his* house. I doubt Donnelly had as many secrets as he thought he did."

"Twelve years is a long time to work for someone like John Donnelly," I said. "There must have been something that made it worth the abuse."

"His secretary has been with him twenty-one years," Jack said. "But the answer is easy. Money. He pays the people who make his life easiest and most organized. His attorney, his secretary, and his house manager."

Carver pulled up the financials for José and Martha.

"Holy cow," I said. "They make more than all of us combined."

"That's because we work for the people," Carver said. "Fortunately, Michelle's salary allows me to live the life I've become accustomed to."

"Amen," I said. "What about Kevin Fischer?"

"His financials will take a bit of time," Carver said. "He's got things protected. And he has hidden assets."

"I told you he was suspicious," I said to Jack.

"There's a difference between being suspicious and being a murderer," he said. "But we'll take a close look at him. I'm not sure of his motive though. He just lost a major client, and he wasn't left anything in the will."

"Maybe Donnelly's client list will go to Fischer," I said.

"Could be," Jack said.

"So outside of the girlfriend and house manager," Carver said, "Who else might want this guy dead?"

"Everybody," Jack and I said together.

"He's got two ex-wives and had multiple relationships," I said. "He got a woman pregnant and paid her off so she and the kid would get out of his life. He's got four adult children with his exes. His own attorney used to be his partner until they got into it and split up. Then there's any number of his cases and the death threats to go along with them."

"Give me half an hour, and I'll compile all the data," Carver said, his flingers flying over the keyboard. He was talking to Magnolia under his breath and the conversation seemed to be pretty intense.

I decided to take the autopsy files to the chair in the corner and read through them. I started with Dana Martin's since she was the most recent and her murder was most similar to Donnelly's.

I read through the file and made notes. "You've perfected your technique each time, haven't you?"

"What's that?" Jack asked.

I hadn't even realized he'd taken the chair across from me and was going through the case files of the other victims.

"Just talking to myself," I said. "Carver, can Magnolia multitask?"

"Sure thing," he said. "She's programmed to listen to your commands. Just tell her what you want her to do."

"Thanks," I said. "Magnolia, put on screen all information on Dana Martin, including financials."

"You got something?" Jack asked.

"Just trying to get to know her a little better. Why was she a target?" I asked. "She's a young, attractive woman. Early thirties. She's been married two years to her second husband, and she's got two small kids. She's a trauma nurse at Heartland General and works nights. She and her husband pull in a good living. They've got a nice house, and are involved in their local church. But the killer targets her. He watches her and knows her work schedule, and he abducts her in the parking garage when she's going off shift."

"According to the case file," Jack said. "The husband reported her missing right away when she didn't make it home before he left for work. In his statement he said she always got home about seven fifteen and then he'd leave for work. She'd get the kids packed up and take them to daycare, and then she'd come back home and sleep."

"That's a rough schedule," I said. "It's bad enough to hardly see each other, but add in two small kids and I can't imagine. Maybe they were having trouble."

"The detective in charge looked at the husband hard. But there was nothing to tie him with. He also spent quite a bit of time looking at the ex. Apparently the first marriage ended because she had an affair."

"With husband number two?" I asked.

"No, someone she worked with at the hospital," he said. "The trail went cold. There were no cameras in the parking garage, and there were no witnesses who saw her, or anyone, leaving. Her car was missing from the parking garage, so they could only assume he drove her out in her own car like with Donnelly. There were no calls for ransom. Search parties were formed and they combed miles and miles of territory. Two days later her body was found on top of city hall."

"What about her vehicle?"

"They didn't find her vehicle for five weeks. It was parked in long-term parking at the airport. Her purse was in the back seat, everything still intact."

"Her bra was missing," I said.

"What?"

"In the medical examiner's report, he itemizes her clothing. She was wearing the scrubs she'd left the hospital in. But she wasn't wearing a bra. Just like Donnelly was missing his belt."

"Souvenirs," Jack said. "In Pritchett's police report, there was a notation that his wallet was never found. They had credit cards and the bank monitored to see if charges would show up, but they never did. And Carlisle's shoes were missing. His co-workers said he habitually wore white sneakers when he was doing surgeries. There were no sneakers in his locker at the hospital or his home closet."

"Did Cole find anything in the Porsche?"

"They found the other champagne bottle in the passenger seat, and blood in the back seat."

"Blood?" I asked. "How much blood?"

"Not much," he said. "But the lab said it matched Donnelly's."

"He had a cut on his finger," I said. "Pretty deep. But the blow to the back of the head didn't break the skin. Anything else?"

"There was a briefcase and trench coat in the trunk, along with the missing suit jacket. Donnelly's wallet was inside the coat."

"No cell phone?" I asked.

"No, but that'd be the first thing I'd get rid of. If someone reported him missing, it's too easy to triangulate location by using your cell phone."

"Something else I noticed in the ME's report," I said. "The knife used to disembowel the victim is similar, if not the same. Our notations are almost exact. Given the direction of the cut, it's most likely the killer is right-handed. And given the depth of the cut, I'd say the knife is no longer than four inches, very sharp, and with a smooth blade. There are no variations in how deep the cuts across the abdomen were, which tells me the knife was probably all the way in, but it was sharp enough for him to cut in one smooth stroke. But the interesting part is I found rope fibers inside the cut. Just like the medical examiner found rope fibers inside the cut on Dana Martin."

"I'd say that makes the link between the two a pretty high probability that the killer was one and the same."

"You guys want to see this?" Carver asked.

"Oh, I'd forgotten you were here," Jack said. "It's been hours."

"I could've gone faster if I'd had a snack," he said. "Maybe an ice cream bar. Or a Hot Pocket."

"Now I see where Doug gets it," I said.

"Kevin Fischer's financials had so many protections and passcodes I started to wonder if he was working for the CIA. But it just turns out he's got some shady dealings. If he's not the killer I think a call to the IRS is in order. But Fischer's financials aren't the only interesting things Magnolia has found. Check this out."

The whiteboard lit up as pictures and information were added rapidly. Lines connected people and places, so it looked like a map. It reminded me of a spider's web, and in the center was John Donnelly.

"Magnolia found your connection," Carver said. "Dana Martin used to work at Virginia Hospital Center before she transferred to Richmond and started a new life. The same hospital as Dr. Steven Carlisle."

"Let me guess," I said. "He's the guy she was having an affair with."

"Bingo," Carver said.

"The affair would explain the betrayal aspect of the way she and Donnelly were killed. Carlisle was found in his garage. He was upright and his hands tied so they were straight out. But there are subtle differences."

"Killers perfect their message and skill the more they kill," Carver said.

"Now we just need to figure out how Carlisle and Martin are connected to John Donnelly," I said.

"We'll talk to his secretary tomorrow," Jack said. "She's got all the information on threats he received and all of his case files."

"He's old school," Carver said. "All of his case files are on paper. I hacked into his office computer and other than general client information, there's nothing in there."

"What about the first victim? I asked. "Any connections there?"

"Actually," Carver said. "I've run into a little snag with the first victim. Carson Pritchett didn't exist three years before he was murdered. Now someone went to a lot of trouble to make it look like he existed—they gave him a background, parents, both deceased of course, an education and medical and dental records. But it's too clean. I've seen enough files like that before to recognize government interference."

"What do you mean?" I asked.

"He was witness protection?" Jack asked, catching on before I did.

"Yes," Carver said. "And even I can't get into those sealed records without calling in some massive favors. But in his new life, Carson Pritchett was head of the American Donor Society."

"That's a medical connection at least," I said. "It also seems like a job you'd need to be qualified for.

Not just something you could be plugged into fresh into WITSEC."

"I'd guess he was a doctor in his previous life," Carver said.

"A doctor, a nurse, and the head of the largest organ donor organization in the country," Jack said.

"Yeah, something stinks about the whole thing, and John Donnelly is the connecting factor."

"Speaking of things that stink," Jack said. "I've got a package that had a dead cat in it. I'm sending it to the lab tomorrow to check for fingerprints and to pull DNA if they can, but I took a picture of the label so you could run it. It's got a return address and I want you to see what you can find out about the postmark. It's pretty faded, but I figure Magnolia is up to the task."

"Sure am, sugar," she purred.

Jack shot Carver a look, but Carver just grinned like a fool.

"Did the other victims show signs of torture like Donnelly?" Carver asked.

"Yes," I said. "Extensive on the two men. Dana Martin's injuries weren't as bad. Bruising and lacerations for the most part, and she showed signs of burns, though not with a cattle prod like Donnelly. I looked at the photos and it looked like a branding iron of some sort."

"I read the autopsy report on Martin," Carver said. "I think the killer had a harder time hurting a woman. That's the only explanation for the differences in injuries. When I run something like that through my profiling program, there's a high probability that the killer has an important woman in his life—a wife, a daughter."

I nodded and said, "Cause of death for all three victims was strangulation. No signs of sexual assault for Martin. I wasn't able to decipher what was used for branding. Could've been a ring or a keychain."

"I'll see if Magnolia can get a better look," he said.

"Martin, Carlisle, and Donnelly had natural-fiber rope burns around the neck, wrists and feet. Pritchett had synthetic-fiber rope burns."

"He adjusted his technique with each victim. The natural-fiber rope, the high-gauge wire, even the blade he used to gut them—all of those things are as common as you get. Most people around here probably have that stuff in their garages or toolboxes. He used the rope to strangle each victim instead of his hands. Using his hands would've been too intimate. He wanted to get the job done."

I flinched. I couldn't help myself. I knew what it felt like to have someone's hands around my throat, squeezing until the pressure built and my lungs burned from trying to gasp for air. But gasping for air was impossible. Only the instinct to breathe. And that's when the fear and panic come. Because it's that moment you know you're going to die, and all you can do is wait until the urge to breathe disappears altogether and everything goes black.

I'd somehow managed to live. I don't know why or how. But I did know it's a horror I'd never wish on my worst enemy.

Jack squeezed my shoulder as he came to stand next to me. "So are you saying you don't think he's a typical serial killer? He's not doing it because he enjoys it."

"I think he's doing it because it fulfills his agenda," Carver said. "Somehow, those four people wronged him, and in his mind the only punishment for their crimes is death. Even the way he tortured them doesn't adhere to someone who enjoyed the work. There's anger there. He's not a pro. A pro knows where to cut, where to hit, to do the most damage while keeping them alive long enough to feel the pain. The torture of these victims was almost an afterthought until he was ready to kill them."

"They never did find the kill site for any of the victims," Carver continued. "There were no cameras in the alley where Pritchett was found. It's not a great neighborhood, so there were no witnesses that came forward. People said it was like a ghost did it. One minute there was no body, and the next, Pritchett was tied upright to a chain link fence, his arms splayed and the whole front of him bloody.

"Carlisle's body was found hanging from the rafters in his garage—again, upright and arms splayed wide. His security system had been disengaged. There were no prints or DNA found other than Carlisle's, so police think the killer was there just long enough to leave the body and disappear. But no neighbors saw anything except for a ninety-two-year-old woman at the end of the block who said she saw a white truck parked in the driveway of the house next door, but no one was living there at the time so she didn't know who it belonged to.

"Police are baffled as to how Dana Martin's body ended up on top of city hall and strapped to the radio tower. The building has twenty-four-hour security guards and a system. But the security cameras went out for thirty-two minutes, and the security guard thought it was due to lightning in the area, so he called maintenance to get things up and running again. By the time the system rebooted, Dana Martin had been tied to the radio tower and her guts spilled all over the roof."

"Can you put the four crime scene photos side by side on the screen?" I asked.

"Do bears poop in the woods?" Carver asked.

I watched as the photos appeared on the wall. Pritchett, his lifeless body upright against a chain link fence, his arms splayed wide, his guts spilled open. Carlisle, hanging from the rafters in his garage, his arms strung up so he looked like a marionette, his guts at his feet. Dana Martin, her body fragile and tiny pressed against the metal of the radio tower, her arms stretched to each side, her abdomen splayed open. And John Donnelly, upright on the scarecrow pole how we'd found him two days before.

"Judas," I said. "But who did they betray?"

"We need those case files," Jack said. "I think the answer is in there."

10

I SET MY ALARM AT SIX SO I COULD HIT SNOOZE twice before I absolutely had to get up and get in the shower. The snooze button was part of my essential morning routine. I didn't understand people who could just wake up—like Jack.

By the time my second alarm went off, the smell of coffee was wafting beneath my nose, and the aroma was making my heart beat a little faster. Jack always brought me coffee in the mornings and set it on the nightstand. I seriously had no idea how I'd functioned all the years before Jack. He made life much more enjoyable.

I halfway scooted into a sitting position and reached for the mug, my eyes still closed. The shower was running in the bathroom, and I knew that Jack had turned it on for me so I didn't have to wait for it to warm up. He really was the best.

I managed to find my way into the shower, and I drank the rest of my coffee while letting the hot water hit me in the back of the head. And then I remembered I'd washed my hair the day before and hadn't planned on getting it wet this morning.

I had to go straight to the funeral home as soon as the will reading was finished, so I chose black trousers with a wide belt and a pin-striped button-down shirt. I half dried my hair and pulled it into a loose bun on top of my head. I'd left my nice black booties at the office, still covered in mud, so I slipped on my black ballet flats and hoped it wasn't supposed to rain.

I headed downstairs and heard voices in the kitchen, but I slowed down when I heard mention of Floyd Parker's name.

"I'm just saying," Carver said, "he's not someone to underestimate. He's not your regular small-town hick reporter. The guy's got a brain. And he's got connections. Not as good as yours, but he's got some. He's getting some big-time donations—"

"You ran his financials?" Jack asked. "Carver—"

"Don't *Carver* me in that tone. You're my friend. And no one is going to catch me. I built the program. What I'm telling you is that there are people in the state of Virginia who want to see you fail. You've got the ear of the governor, and you've got friends in high places in D.C., including me. That doesn't make sense to people sitting on the other side of the aisle. Why would a sheriff in King George County have such influential people in his pockets unless he had higher ambitions?"

"You know that's not true," Jack said. "And I don't really care what people say. My friends are my friends, and not because of who they are or what positions they hold. And if somebody is lining Floyd's pockets to beat me and keep me from higher aspirations, then it's money wasted. Floyd still has to win over the voters, and he's not going to do that."

"He doesn't have to win over the voters," Carver said, his tone serious. "He just has to discredit you so badly that the voters have no other choice in who to vote for. The election is in a couple of weeks. All I'm saying is be careful."

"I always am," Jack said.

I figured I'd lingered at the bottom of the stairs long enough, but Carver's warning worried me. Floyd had always been a nuisance, but it ran much deeper than him disliking Jack or being mad at me for tossing him aside all those years ago. He was jealous of Jack, and he always had been, even in school. And Floyd had spent much too much of his life trying to come out on top and failing.

I grabbed my black leather jacket from the coat closet, and made enough noise so they'd know I was there. And then I went in the kitchen.

"There she is," Carver said, his grin infectious. "It's always a pleasure to see you in the mornings, Jaye. So bright eyed and bushy tailed."

"Shut up, Carver," I said, and I took the to-go mug of coffee Jack handed me. "What does that even mean? I'm not a squirrel."

Carver was a morning person like Jack. Actually, Carver was an all-the-time person. His brain and energy functioned on a different plane than the rest of us mere mortals. He was always alert.

"If you hadn't hit snooze so many times," Carver said. "Maybe you'd have gotten down here in time for breakfast, and I wouldn't have had to eat all your bacon."

"I'm used to not getting to eat with the Carver boys in the house," I said. "I'll get donuts on the way to the office." I hadn't forgotten that I'd promised Tom I'd pay him a visit during the week, and somehow single-handedly buy enough donuts to keep him in business.

"We've got to go," Jack said to Carver. "It's a busy morning of witnessing hopes and dreams flushed down the toilet."

"You always get to have all the fun," Carver said, pouting a little. "Maybe one day I'll decide to work in the field."

Jack grabbed his keys from the bowl on the foyer table and laughed. "Just because they give you a gun to carry doesn't mean you should use it. I've seen you shoot. You're much deadlier behind a keyboard."

"Hey, that's not fair," Carver said, following us to the front door in his wheelchair. "I needed a new prescription for my glasses last time we went to the range. I could barely see the target."

"You couldn't hit the broad side of a barn," Jack said, ushering me out the front door. "It's just fortunate for you you're married to Michelle. Now that's a woman who can shoot."

Jack closed the door in time to hear Carver swear, and he grinned all the way to the truck. We rode the entire way to John Donnelly's house without speaking. The radio was on low in the background, but I wasn't big on conversation in the mornings, and Jack seemed lost in thought. I didn't know whether or not I should bring up the conversation I'd overheard him and Carver having, so I watched the landscape pass through my window and tried not to let thoughts of Floyd ruin my day.

There were several other cars parked in front of the house when we finally pulled in, and I could hear the yelling as soon as we got out of the car.

"Seems like it's going well so far," I said, glancing at Jack. "I hope we haven't missed too much."

"They haven't even started yet," Jack said. "This is just the pregame show."

I was glad I'd remembered my jacket. There was a damp chill in the air. I wasn't a fan of cold rain, but I wasn't opposed to it if it meant the Halloween block party would be cancelled, so I was keeping my fingers crossed.

The front door stood open, and when we stepped into the foyer, Kevin Fischer was there waiting for us. There was a man I could only assume was his security guard standing just off to the side of the door.

"Sheriff, Dr. Graves," he said, shaking our hands. "I'm glad you could make it. We're just waiting on a couple of more people and then we can get started."

"It sounds like something is already started," Jack said, nodding to the direction where the screaming was coming from.

"Kimmie doesn't like having people in her house," he said. "Especially ex-wives. And she's had a couple of mimosas this morning, which makes her extra pleasant to be around. I will say Isabelle Rhodes had the right idea. She called me this morning and said she'd decided not to cart her son halfway across the country for the whims of John Donnelly. She said they'd survived this long without him, and they didn't need or want anything from him now that he was dead. I didn't have the heart to tell her he didn't leave them anything."

"It's probably for the best," I said, wincing as Kimmie's voice carried through the house. "This is the last place a nine-year-old boy needs to be."

There was a knock on the open door, and Michael Donnelly stepped into his father's house, gazing across the wide-open expanse of white. "I always thought this house was cold and ugly, but I haven't been here since I was a kid. It's still cold and ugly."

He smiled wryly and then saw me standing between Jack and Kevin.

"Dr. Graves," he said, coming to me directly and shaking my hand. "It's nice to see you again. I didn't know you would be here."

"We were a last-minute addition," I said.

"I extended the invitation to Dr. Graves and Sheriff Lawson," Kevin said. "On the chance something is revealed that can help them find your father's killer during the reading of the will."

"Of course," Michael said and then he introduced himself to Jack. "Michael Donnelly."

"Jack Lawson," Jack said. "I'm sorry for your loss."

"I appreciate it," Michael said. "Is Mom here?" he asked Kevin.

"Yes, she and your sister are in the sitting room with everyone else."

"How's she holding up?" Michael asked.

"She hasn't killed Kimmie yet, if that's what you're asking," Kevin said, his mouth tilted in a smile at one corner.

"Mom is the least of Kimmie's worries," Michael said.

"True," Kevin said. "I told her if she'd behave herself I'd send her and Jilly on one of those riverboat cruises they keep talking about. So far, no one has thrown a punch."

"That's probably as good as you can hope for," Michael said. "Unless Kimmie punches first. Then you'd better just get out of the way." Michael laughed and threw an arm around his godfather's shoulder. "I'll go in and see if I can get things to settle down."

"He's a good kid," Kevin said, after he'd left. "Jilly and I were never blessed with children, so Michael and his sisters are like our own. We've thrown them parties and helped with graduations, showers, and weddings. We'd take them on vacation when they were children. We were there for every Christmas and birthday."

"When John never was," I finished for him.

"When John never was," he agreed. "Some men aren't meant to be fathers. I found it cruel that something I wanted to be so much was given to someone who didn't want the job. But we play with the cards life deals us and move on."

If there wasn't that underlying level of car salesman, most people would probably think Kevin Fischer was a pretty good guy. But then I thought about his financial dealings and the people he was screwing out of their retirement and investments and was glad I'd learned to trust my instincts.

"Excuse me," a soft voice said.

A thin, tidy-looking woman in a gray suit and excellent shoes stood stiff as a board just outside the doorway. She was blond and her hair was swooped up in a twist on the back of her head, and her makeup was tasteful and subtle. She was somewhere in her late forties or early fifties, and she reminded me of Grace Kelly.

"Martha," Kevin said, his smile genuine as he went to greet her. "Come in, come in. It's always wonderful to see you."

Her gaze crossed over us briefly before her attention turned back to Kevin. "I almost didn't come," she confessed. "The firm is in an uproar, and I have a million things to do. I don't see why it's necessary that I'm here."

"It was John's wish that you would be," he said. "I promise this shouldn't take too long. How have you been doing through all of this?"

"It's been difficult," she said. "A shock. I still can't wrap my mind around the fact that he's gone. I don't really know what to do with myself." The voices in the other room were growing louder again and she looked in that direction. "I really don't even know what I'm doing here."

"You were very important to John," Kevin said. "Don't ever doubt that."

She laughed then, a tinkling sound that was quite pleasant. I couldn't place her accent. Not American, but it sounded like she'd tried hard to flatten her speech and sound like everyone else.

"I don't know if I was important to John, but I tried my hardest to make him think he could never survive without me," she said, her smile infectious. "If you only knew how many times he'd threatened to fire me over the last twenty years."

"Sounds like a normal day at the office to me," Kevin said, patting her shoulder gently. "I want to introduce you to Sheriff Lawson and Dr. Graves. They're investigating John's murder."

"Oh, of course," she said. "It's a pleasure to meet you. Have you found anything?"

"It's still early in the investigation," Jack said, "But we're making progress."

"Let me know if I can be of any help," she said. "I can only think that someone finally made good on their threats. The very nature of his career made him a target."

"I'd like to speak with you about that once we're wrapped up here. We were told you kept any threats he received."

"I have a drawer full," she said. "He would never let me call the police. He said it wasn't a big deal, and no one would go through with it. But I could tell it was wearing on him over the last couple of years. I was worried about him over these last months. He wasn't looking well."

"Why don't we go ahead and get this over with," Kevin said. "We're not expecting anyone else, and then you can get Sheriff Lawson the death threat information."

"Of course," Martha said, nodding to Jack.

Kevin guided Martha to the living area at the back of the house, and Jack and I trailed behind them. It was as white and sterile as all the other rooms I'd seen, with the exception of a contemporary painting in bright splashes of pinks and reds that hung over the fireplace. It took me a moment to realize it was a portrait of Kimmie. It didn't do her any favors.

But it was the view of the outside that almost made up for the sterility of the inside. The pool and lush greenery were an oasis, and then there was the golf course practically in their backyard.

The security guard came in behind us and then went to stand against the wall where he could see everyone.

"Who's he?" Kimmie asked, pointing at the security guard. She poured herself a glass of champagne and added a splash of orange juice to the top.

"He's from my firm," Kevin said. "To make sure everyone is on their best behavior."

There was a delicate snort that came from one of the couches, but no one paid it much attention. Jack and I stayed at the back of the room, so we could see everyone.

There was a glass table at the opposite end of the room that Kevin had made a sort of temporary desk. His briefcase lay on top, and he took a seat in an uncomfortable-looking chair that probably cost a fortune.

"If I could have everyone's attention," he said, "We can get through this quickly and everyone can go about their day."

"It's about time," Kimmie said, taking a seat on a white leather bench and propping stiletto boots on the glass table in front of it. She'd chosen a black skinsuit that didn't leave much to the imagination, and she'd adorned it with a sparkling belt that hung at her hips and matching earrings that hung down to her shoulders. I wasn't sure if she was about to dance backup for Beyoncé or join the Avengers.

A woman with striking Native American features turned and looked down her nose at Kimmie. I recognized Anna Donnelly from the photograph on our whiteboard at home.

"Kevin, let's please continue," she said. "I don't know why we had to do this all together."

"John insisted," Kevin said.

"Of course he did," Anna said, her lips thinning as she took the hand of the younger version of herself sitting next to her.

"Enough," Kimmie said. "I've got plans this afternoon and I need everyone out of here. Stop stalling, Kevin. I swear I don't know why John kept you on after you split the firm."

"Maybe someone should hide the booze," the woman next to Anna said. "I think someone has had enough."

None of John's children looked like him, which they all probably found fortunate every time they looked in the mirror.

"Stop being a whiny bitch, Abbie," Kimmie said, downing her glass.

"Just ignore her, honey," Christine Donnelly said from the opposite couch. She sat between Michael and Madison, her own children. "She's just jealous because she was never anything more than a live-in. One of many. If you ask me, it's Julie who should be here. She was the only person John actually gave a damn about.

The champagne flute bulleted from Kimmie's hand and smashed against the wall behind Christine's head before any of us could anticipate. And the shrieks were toddler tantrum worthy. Jack had his hand on his weapon, but it was Kevin's voice who cut through the noise.

"Ms. Kloss, you will be forcibly removed from this house if your behavior doesn't change, and I'm sure you wouldn't like to add an assault charge on top of things. Now sit down, and shut up so we can get this over with."

Kimmie let loose with a profanity-ridden tirade, but finally took her seat.

"I know that these aren't ideal circumstances," Kevin said. "But my instructions come from John directly, and this is being recorded per John's instructions." He hit a remote, and it was then I noticed the video camera set up in the corner. "In attendance are Anna Donnelly, and her two children, Abigail and Charlene. Christine Donnelly, and her two children, Madison and Michael. Kimberly Kloss. José Sosa. And Martha Callum."

Martha was standing near us against the wall, and José sat alone near the French doors.

"Also in attendance are me, attorney for the deceased, Kevin Fischer. Julian Starr, also with my firm, and Sheriff Jack Lawson and Dr. J.J. Graves. We're missing two individuals who denied the summons to attend this morning. Isabelle Rhodes and her son, Samuel."

There were several murmurs as those in attendance tried to discover the identity of the missing party.

"I'm sorry," Christine finally said. "But who in the world is Isabelle Rhodes?"

Kevin sighed and steepled his hands on top of the desk. "A decade or so ago, she was a woman John had a relationship with. The relationship resulted in a child. Samuel."

"No way," I heard several of them say as chaos erupted.

"I have a brother?" Michael asked. "Why weren't we ever told?"

Kevin lifted his hands to try to get everyone to calm down. "Your father and Ms. Rhodes made an arrangement. He paid her a settlement to move and deny him as the father. She took it and moved to Arizona to raise her son."

"I really hate that son of a bitch," Abbie said, her face pale.

"Can we meet him?" Madison asked. "He should know he has a brother and sisters."

"I can certainly make an introduction," Kevin said. "But just be prepared for Isabelle to deny the request. She didn't want anything to do with the will reading today or anything John might have left her."

"Good for her," Anna said, nodding her head, and then she looked at Christine. "We will try to reach out. We've had each other all these years. She's had no one."

My respect for the Donnelly ex-wives had increased tenfold. They were strong, independent women who'd suffered at the hand of John Donnelly, and they'd somehow managed to make their own family.

"Martha," Kevin called out. "You don't have to stand. There's a seat here."

It was obvious Martha was trying to blend into the walls, but she nodded and walked to the front of the room and took a seat on a chair identical to the one Kevin was sitting in.

"I'd like to start by saying that I've been John's friend and attorney for a long time, and I advised him against this. But when he has his mind set on something, there's nothing anyone can do to change it. You all know this, of course. But John came to me last month to get his affairs in order. He didn't give me the specifics, but he felt he had very little time left. We know now, after his autopsy, that he had several health issues he wouldn't have been with us much longer."

"Are you saying my father changed his will a month ago?" Abbie asked.

"Yes," Kevin said. "He wanted to make sure all his affairs were in order. He made the changes, I witnessed them, and then he sealed it in this envelope. He told me not to submit it to probate until after his death.

"The contents of John's assets are quite extensive," he continued. "They include this house, which he owns outright. Three vacation homes, rental property, a stake in a Manhattan apartment complex, vehicles, stocks, bonds, bank accounts, art, and jewelry worth an estimated one hundred million dollars."

The room got very still, and there were several exchanged glances. Kimmie's smile was smug. José didn't move a muscle.

"He left instructions that I'm to read a letter he wrote to all of you, and then I'll read the contents of his will. So…" Kevin unsealed the envelope and pulled out two sheets of paper. He quickly skimmed the first page and then began to read.

If you're listening to Kevin read this letter, then you were of some importance to me, either in the past or the present. I always thought I would live forever. Hell, maybe the doctors are wrong about this whole thing and I still might. But the thought of all of you being in a room together gives me some pleasure here at the end. I'll confess, I wish I could be a fly on the wall.

Maybe you're all expecting an apology. I probably owe you one. Who the hell knows. But I don't have any regrets in my life. I am who I am. Which is why none of you should be surprised with the changes made to my will. It's time everyone goes and lives the life they deserve to live. I don't know if you'll miss me or not. I can't particularly say I care if you do. But despite your feelings for me, good or bad, I want to say you're free of me. And try not to be too angry.

Yours Truly,

John

"Without further ado…" Kevin said, flipping to the second page, "…I, John Frances Donnelly, being of sound mind and body, hereby leave all cash assets, including stocks, bonds, and bank accounts in their entirety to my secretary, Martha Callum."

The gasps almost drowned out Kevin's voice, but he kept reading.

"My ownership in any real estate or developments, I leave in its entirety to Martha Callum. My home and all the contents within, I also leave to Martha Callum. All other assets in my name, I leave in their entirety to Martha Callum."

"You can't be serious," Madison said, coming to her feet. "That unbelievable bastard. After everything he put us through."

"Sit down, Maddie," Michael said, pulling on his sister's hand. "We never needed anything of his. We all have our trust funds that can't be touched. That won't change anything now."

"It's the principle," she said, her face white with anger. "What about Mom?"

Christine started laughing uncontrollably and Anna joined in. "God, it's just like him, isn't it?" Christine said. "Don't worry about us. We've both made excellent investments over the years. I guess we should thank Kevin for that."

Kevin looked relieved and nodded, and then he said, "There's more. To my wives, I hope you're not too disappointed, but you got more than your fair share in the divorces. To my children, you've all lived a life of luxury with the best educations money could buy. Go use them. To Kimmie, you're young, and anything I've given to you as a gift is yours. I'm sure you'll bounce back quickly and find a man who's dumb enough to marry you. To Martha, I'd advise you to keep José on while you're trying to decide what to do with the house and its contents. Whether you decide to keep him on after that is up to you. He's very knowledgeable. To José, I've set aside a severance package in case Martha has no need of your services."

I was watching Martha Callum. She hadn't moved. And her face had drained of all color so it was almost as white as the chair she was sitting in. Everyone's gaze turned to her, and then Kimmie erupted.

"No!" she screamed. "I'm going to fight this. He was ill. Out of his mind! I won't have it," she said. "He promised me. He promised we'd get married. He promised this would all be mine. Do you know the things I let that man do to me? He was so old. And now you're telling me he's just going to leave everything to some nobody secretary?"

Kimmie's gaze lasered in on Martha and she took a step forward. "Were you screwing him too like that bitch Julie? Were you?"

Kevin hurried over and put himself in between Kimmie and Martha. "You have a right to your anger," Kevin said. "But it is what it is, and there's nothing to fight. Don't make things worse. These were his wishes, and it's all laid out quite simply. Ms. Kloss, you'll have until five o'clock today to remove your personal belongings from the home. The Manhattan apartment is in your name, but I must remind you that the payments become yours as well. If you'd like, I can recommend a realtor so you can put it on the market.

Kimmie spun on her heel and flounced out of the room. I could hear her heels clicking all the way up the stairs.

Kevin rolled his eyes and then turned to Martha. "There are some papers I'm going to need you to sign. You need to make a decision on whether or not you'd like to keep José on to help you with the house. Do you want him to stay?"

She nodded wordlessly. "At least until the house goes on the market. I can't stay here."

"I understand," Kevin said.

But it wasn't Kevin I'd been watching. It was José. And though his face was passively blank, his fists were balled so tight I could see the white of his knuckles.

Kevin looked at the children and Anna and Christine. "I truly am sorry," he said. "I'll be here in the house today until it's vacated. But I'm happy to answer any questions you might have."

"I think I'd like a drink," Anna said.

"Come on," Christine said. "My house is closest. We could all use a drink."

"This is awkward," I whispered to Jack.

"What do you want to bet Kimmie tries to leave with everything but the kitchen sink?"

I snickered. "Let's get out of here."

Jack and I walked over to where Martha was still sitting. She hadn't moved, and she was staring down at her hands.

"Ms. Callum," Jack said.

"Martha," she said. "Please."

Jack nodded. "I know this came as a surprise. But I really need to speak with you about Mr. Donnelly's murder. The more time that passes, the more likely his killer is to go uncaught. Contact me as soon you've had time to let this settle."

Her gaze met Jack's and there was a steely strength in it that reminded me she'd worked for John Donnelly for twenty-one years. She was nobody's pushover.

"I'm fine," she said. "I was just caught off guard for a moment. But you're right. Meet me at the office at noon, and we'll go through the files. And I know you're going to ask for case files, but I have to tell you because of the sensitive nature of some of John's current cases, you're going to need a warrant."

"I'll have one," Jack said. "I'll see you in a couple of hours. Congratulations, by the way."

"Thank you," she said, coming to her feet. "I'd like to say I don't deserve it, but I sure as hell do. I haven't had a vacation in years, and there were times I wanted to kill him myself. But I'm sorry about what happened to him. I read about it in the paper. No one should have to die like that."

"No," Jack agreed. "What are you going to do now?"

"I don't know," she said. "But I don't think I'll stay here. My kids are grown and scattered around, but I've got family in Texas. I'll probably end up there. I'm tired of the winters here."

11

I'd have liked to play cop all day with Jack, but I had a job, and it was the kind of job where you couldn't really leave people waiting, so Jack dropped me at the funeral home on his way to the station.

"Call me when you need a ride," he said.

"I should be good for a while. What are you going to do about Dr. Park?"

"I'm heading out now to meet him at his office," he said. "Hopefully, he can squeeze me in between Botox injections."

"If you come back with your face looking like a Ken doll I'm withholding sex."

"Good to know where your level of tolerance ends," he said, smiling. "Stay out of trouble."

"You too," I said, leaning over for a kiss. "Keep me updated." I hopped out of the truck and waved as he drove off.

I let myself in through the kitchen door, hung my jacket in the mudroom, and then headed straight for the coffeepot. Someone had already made some, but the pot was cold so I started a fresh one.

"Oh, Dr. Graves," Lily said, coming in behind me. "We were wondering when you'd be here. We got three bodies in this morning, and we're expecting two more this afternoon. With John Donnelly already in the cooler, we'll be at our max capacity."

"Three this morning?" I asked, surprised. "Where'd they come from? Have the families been in touch?"

"Emmy Lu has all the details," she said.

Lily looked slightly frazzled, and she never looked frazzled.

"Y'all should have called me," I said.

"It wouldn't have done any good. We knew you were at the will reading. Besides, all this happened in just the last half hour. The hospital called and then bodies and people started showing up. It was a madhouse. I think Sheldon was crying."

I sighed and handed her a cup of coffee before doctoring my own. Sheldon tended to get emotional when things got too stressful.

"How are the bodies?" I asked.

"We haven't gotten them cleaned or prepped yet," she said. "There's a family in the salon, and I was just about to go meet with them. Had you rather do that? I know I don't normally meet with clients, but I figured I was the better option until Sheldon got himself under control."

"Good point," I said. "You take the family. I need to meet with Emmy Lu and then I'll get started on the bodies. If we've got more coming in this afternoon I don't want to get too behind."

I took my coffee and headed into the main part of the funeral home. My grandparents had wanted to make it look as much like a home as possible, so the foyer was wide and welcoming with soft colors, rich woods, and fresh flowers. There were two viewing parlors downstairs and two more upstairs, each done in a different color, and there was a smaller chapel on the first floor as well with a stained-glass window. The chapel gave me the creeps so I rarely went in there. There were also two salons on the first floor we used to meet with clients, and at the far back of the funeral home was the casket room, where we kept a good selection in stock for people to choose from.

To the left side of the entryway was a glassed-in office where Emmy Lu Stout held down the fort. She was a dozen years older than me and had lived in Bloody Mary all her life. She'd married her high school sweetheart and given birth to five boys before her husband had decided to leave her for a bank teller hardly old enough to vote.

When she'd come looking for a job, I couldn't turn her down. I'd never been able to afford a receptionist before, so it was new territory for me. But now that I had her, I didn't know how I'd gone on all this time without her. I understood exactly why John Donnelly had left his fortune to his secretary.

"Thank the Lord you're here," Emmy Lu said, coming out of her office. "You hate to say business is hopping in our line of work, but it's been nonstop for the last hour. My ears are ringing, I've had so many phone calls."

Emmy Lu had babysat me when I was a teenager, and she looked exactly the same except that she was a little wider in the hips and she had crow's feet. She was still cute as a button and had an infectious smile. Her dark hair was piled on top of her head and practically crackling with energy, and she had two pens stuck in it. One of her earrings was missing. I assumed she'd taken it off to talk on the phone.

"The hospital started releasing the bodies of the tornado victims, so that's why we got swamped. Henry and Jessica Lassiter came in first. Father and daughter."

"Oh, man," I said, squeezing my hands around my cup. "I was hoping I wouldn't pull that one. I hate it when it's a kid."

"Me too," she said. "The mom is a wreck. She's in the parlor with her mom and her oldest daughter."

"Lily told me she was meeting with them to go through options. Do me a favor and keep Sheldon away from people today."

"Already on it," she said. "I sent him on an errand to pick up the dry cleaning. Thought the fresh air would do him good. Never saw a grown man cry at the drop of a hat like that."

"Good thinking," I said.

"The Lassiters are ready for embalming, and Mrs. Lassiter brought clothes for the funeral. I've already called Larissa Carol, and she's on standby when you're ready for hair. I've also gotten in touch with Ginny Grainger at the flower shop."

"You're amazing," I said. "Who's our third guest?"

"Lucy Randolph," she said. "The family wants an open casket."

The way she said it made me pause for a second. "And should she have an open casket?"

Emmy Lu grimaced. "She took refuge in her garden shed when the tornado hit. There were lots of sharp things in there. She came to us in pieces."

It was my turn to grimace. But I understood people's grief. They wanted to see their loved ones how they remembered them, but sometimes that just wasn't possible.

"I'll see what I can do, but no promises," I said. "Anything else?"

"That's not enough?"

"Just checking," I said.

"We're scheduled to get two more bodies in this afternoon. I told the hospital to hold off until we could get caught up on our storage situation. And someone from the *Gazette* called wanting to do an interview with you about the upcoming election."

"I'll pass," I said.

"I figured as much. I knew the second the woman started talking Floyd Parker was behind it. Heard you had a run-in with him at Martin's Grocery yesterday."

"I figure everyone has heard by now," I said. "And I didn't even do anything but run over his toes with the buggy."

"Maybe next time you'll get to drive over him with your car instead. His oldest brother graduated with me. He liked to tie firecrackers to cats' tails and light them, and there was a rumor that went around school that he would…" She looked around to make sure no one was listening and I leaned in closer to hear. Her voice dropped to a whisper. "That he would masturbate over their carcasses."

My nose scrunched involuntarily. "Eww," I said.

"Those Parker boys are all charming when they gotta be, but they're bad business."

"And with that bit of information I'll never be able to get out of my head," I said, "I'm going to head down to the lab and get started. Let me know if Lily needs any help. I'll be in touch with the families personally once I'm finished with the bodies."

"What should I do about Sheldon?"

I really wanted to work in the lab alone. I *liked* being alone. I sighed. "When he gets back send him down to me. I'm going to need all the hands I can get today."

"AN AVERAGE of sixty-three people die per year from tornadoes," Sheldon said.

"Interesting," I said, rolling Henry Lassiter from the cooler and over to the embalming table. I didn't glance at the small figure lined up next to him.

I'd decided to give Henry to Sheldon to do since he'd be the easiest of the three. I was going to take Lucy Randolph and see if all the king's horses and all the king's men could put her back together again. It was times like this my medical background really came in handy.

"I've always thought so," Sheldon continued. "Natural disasters are fascinating. For instance, flooding kills more people per year than tornadoes, lightning strikes, and hurricanes combined."

"You're going to do Mr. Lassister," I said, trying to get back on track. "It should be very straightforward. Cause of death was head trauma and bleeding on the brain. He's got some external scratches and bruising, but nothing makeup can't conceal. Can you handle it on your own?"

"Of course," he said, blinking at me owlishly. "I've done a solo embalming before in class. I'm graduating in December."

"Right," I said. "Let me know if you have any problems." I turned my playlist on so I wouldn't have to listen to Sheldon talking. He wasn't necessarily talking to me, but he liked to tell the bodies what he was doing to them and regale them with useless trivia. It weirded me out a little, so music was the best way to go.

I went back into the cooler and rolled Lucy Randolph over to the other embalming table. She was under a white sheet, but I could see the jagged tear across her throat where she'd been decapitated. She had some discoloring in the face, but after I got a good look at the body, I was pretty sure I could make her presentable enough for an open casket—as long as I didn't run out of staples or putty. And as long as she wore something with a high collar.

I pulled the sheet down to her waist and then turned on the ventilator above the table. The hospital had sent over their own records and injury inventory to the body, but I still needed to do my own because bruises could sometimes appear days after death. We always kept a record of bodily injuries in case a family tried to sue for whatever reason.

I grabbed my spray bottle of disinfectant from the shelf and went about disinfecting the face—eyes, nose, mouth, and ears—inside and out. And then I grabbed a razor and shaved her face. It made working with makeup and putty much easier, and it was easier to do now rather than later.

There was something soothing in the process. I'd done it countless times before, but I found myself completely focused on Lucy Randolph. She and her family deserved the best I could give her.

I disinfected the rest of her body as well and then checked her for any remaining signs of rigor. I made sure her limbs bent easily at the joints. If I didn't, the embalming fluid wouldn't go where it was supposed to. I then went about the tedious task of stapling and stitching her back together. Besides the severed head, her left arm, leg, and foot had also been dismembered, and she had several deep slices along her torso and abdomen. Almost like a tractor blade had ripped through her.

It was a painstaking process and it had to be done right, meaning I had to make sure the arteries were connected as well as the tissue, otherwise the embalming would be a mess. By the time I finished,

Sheldon was already hosing out the drains and cleaning his equipment.

"Just cover him and leave him on the table for now," I told him, stretching out the kinks in my neck and back. I'd been hunched over the table for a long time. "I'll do any patchwork and makeup when I do hers, and then we can dress them. Larissa is on call to come and do hair once we're finished. Why don't you go get lunch?"

"I can start on the little girl if you'd like," he said. But I could tell by his expression he was hoping I didn't ask him to. Children affected all of us differently. It was tragic, and I'd learned during my days in the ER if I didn't control those emotions then they would control me, and then I wouldn't be any good to anyone.

"No, I'll get her," I told him. "We've got two more coming in this afternoon, and we're going to need all hands on deck. If you can get with Emmy Lu and get the schedules and all the paperwork ready, that would be a big help. And if you're meeting with any clients today remember what we talked about."

"Be sincere and sympathetic," he repeated. "Don't give them useless information, and just listen if they want to talk."

"Good," I said, praying like crazy that he remembered it. "And wear your black sport coat if you have to meet with clients."

"Did you know wearing black when in mourning goes all the way back to Roman times? They'd wear black togas. But India and China traditionally wear white."

"Interesting," I said. "But since we're in America, go ahead and wear your black sport coat."

He gave me a thumbs-up, and then headed up the stairs to the main part of the funeral home. And then I got back to work. I started by taking a couple of ibuprofen because my lower back was on fire, and then I went about the task of setting the face.

The face had to be perfect. It had to represent in death a familiarity that loved ones could recognize from life. So I made sure the plastic eye caps were in place to make the eyes round again where they'd sunken in death before I glued the eyelids closed. Then I wired the jaw shut so the mouth would stay closed.

I looked at the photo of her in her file—a photo of her alive and well—and I was pleased with the outcome. I put some cream on the eyelids and her lips to keep them from drying out, and then got ready to embalm her.

I had to be careful with the incisions I made for the arterial tube and the drain tube, and I had to make an incision in the groin instead of the neck because of her wounds there. I mixed the chemicals, made my incisions, and started the process. The two gallons of embalming fluid coursing through her veins gave her skin a pinkish and more lifelike hue.

I massaged the fingers and feet to make sure the embalming fluid went everywhere it was supposed to, and then I sutured the incisions I'd made. I didn't even bother to check the time. I knew it was well past lunch by the rumbles in my stomach. But I went ahead and mixed putty and paint and filled in the areas around her neck that needed it. And then I did her makeup, matching the skin tone from her picture and making sure it was smooth all the way down her neck. And then I did her hands as well.

While I had everything out, I did the same thing to Mr. Lassiter, and then I dressed them both in the clothes their loved ones had painstakingly picked out.

When I was finished, I gazed longingly up the stairs. I wanted nothing more than to go outside and breathe in fresh air. But then I looked at the remaining body in the cooler and knew I wasn't going anywhere.

12

I WAS ASLEEP ON MY FEET.

I wasn't sure how long I'd been staring at my computer screen, trying to finish up the paperwork from the day, when I felt Jack's hands on my shoulders.

"Hey," he said, and kissed me on the back of the neck.

"Sorry I didn't call," I said. "I didn't mean to make you wait so long. I could've just stayed the night here."

"You didn't make me wait," he said. "And I'm not letting you sleep here alone. Besides, Emmy Lu told me how busy you were. Let's go home and get you in bed."

I think I whimpered. The thought of sliding between the covers was the best suggestion I'd ever heard.

"Only if you go to bed with me," I said, my speech slurred from exhaustion.

"You got it," he said. "Did you eat today?"

"Are you trying to coddle me?" I asked, letting him lead me from my office through the kitchen and mudroom. He grabbed my leather jacket from the hook, but kept pushing me through the door, locking it behind him.

"Of course I am," he said. "It's in the marriage vows."

"I think you keep adding stuff to it," I said. "Every time I turn around there's some other marriage rule I don't know anything about."

"Maybe you need to go back and read them again," he suggested. "Love, honor, and cherish covers a whole lot of ground."

"Hmm," I said. "Do you think I'm a good wife?" I asked as he tucked me into the passenger side of his Tahoe. The window had been fixed and the inside cleaned up. "I want to be."

"You're the best wife," he said, fastening my seat belt for me. "Remember how you cooked for me and made sure I ate the other day? It's give and take. It's all part of the package. When one of us is down it's up to the other of us to take more care and pull a little more weight. Not because we owe each other or have a system of checks and balances, but because that's what love is."

"You're pretty smart," I said, and then I leaned my head against the new window and promptly fell asleep.

I had a vague recollection of being carried from the car and into the house, and the murmur of voices as Jack carried me upstairs to our bedroom. I remember him undressing me and laying me on cool sheets, and then crawling in beside me to hold me until I drifted off again.

But sometime during the night, my hunger woke me from a sound sleep, and my hand automatically went to the opposite side of the bed. But Jack was gone. He'd left the shades up so the moon shone brightly through the floor-to-ceiling windows, and the tips of the trees swayed with the night breeze.

It was my favorite view in the house, even at night. Being on the third floor made it seem like we were sleeping in the treetops.

I glanced at the clock on the nightstand and saw it was almost three in the morning. I was strangely wide awake, and then my stomach growled again, so I rolled out of bed and found the cashmere robe Jack had gotten me for my birthday draped over the back of the chair by the windows. I sighed as I wrapped it around my naked body and tied the belt. If I could've gotten away with wearing it out of the house I would have. I'd never felt anything more luxurious against my skin.

I crept down the stairs, careful not to wake Doug as I passed the second floor, and I saw the light was already on in the kitchen. And then I burst into tears as I saw the sandwich sitting on a plate and a bottle of water next to it. Jack really was the best husband.

I grabbed the plate and the water and wandered through the house until I came to the office. There was nothing but silence on the other side of the door, but I knew he was in there. I slid open the pocket door, and he looked up at me from behind his desk, his dark eyes piercingly direct.

"Thanks for the sandwich," I said, coming over to sit across from him. "And thanks for taking care of me. It was a brutal day."

"I can only imagine," he said. "It's going to be a brutal week. Five funerals is a lot."

"Four," I said. "Father and daughter are being buried together."

"Ah," he said, understanding in his eyes. "It's good they're together."

I bit into my sandwich to keep the tears from coming again. "What'd you find out today with the case? Anything useful?"

"My conversation with Dr. Park was interesting."

"How so?"

"He knew Donnelly was in bad health, and he performed procedures on him anyway," Jack said.

"He said once when Donnelly was in the office getting Botox injections he had a little heart episode. Donnelly popped an aspirin and refused any kind of medical treatment or a ride to the hospital. Said it was nothing. Park said he told him that anesthesia and surgery weren't a good idea until he went and had his heart checked out, but he said John Donnelly was someone you didn't say no to. At least if you wanted your career and business to survive."

"But we know Donnelly did eventually go to the doctor," I said. "So he must have listened to reason."

"We can only assume. Dr. Park had no knowledge of who Donnelly might have used for a physician, and we haven't been able to find anything in his records."

"That's weird," I said. "Stuff like that usually comes up when Carver runs a search."

"Exactly," Jack said.

"What about Martha Callum?" I asked.

"I like her," Jack said. "She knew exactly the kind of man John Donnelly was, and she's nobody's pushover. But she said Donnelly gave her a job when no one else would, and she had three kids to feed on her own. She said the hours were lousy, his temperament was worse, but with what he was paying her she could tolerate it. She hadn't been kidding about the threats. She had a drawer full of letters and other odds and ends of things he'd been sent over the last twenty years."

"Anything stand out to you?" I asked.

"I haven't been through everything yet, but there was a letter sent from a Richmond post office dated about six years ago. It basically accuses Donnelly and several others of payoffs and false testimony, and then he tells him there's innocent blood on his hands and that the betrayal won't go unpunished. But the real clincher is that he signs the letter with a Bible verse. Acts 1:18–19."

"That's one I haven't memorized," I said dryly, making Jack grin. It was then I noticed he had his Bible out on the desk.

"With the reward he got for his wickedness, Judas bought a field; there he fell headlong, his body burst open and all his intestines spilled out. Everyone in Jerusalem heard about this, so they called that field in their language Akeldama, that is, Field of Blood."

"Okay," I said. "I see where you might connect the dots there. Any idea who it could have come from?"

"Martha had no idea, but I've got case files from around that time flagged for us to go through first. We might have better luck narrowing our search on the other victim—Dana Martin. It might be easier to connect her to Donnelly than the other way around. I've scanned all of the letters into the computer, and Magnolia is going to analyze the handwriting and see if there are any commonalities. I've also got a call in to Dana Martin's husband. There was mention in the police report that Dana had been concerned about a stalker. She felt like someone was watching her, but nothing ever came of it. I wanted to ask her husband if he remembers her getting any letters in the mail. Any tangible threats."

"There's nothing in the police report?" I asked.

"No, but not all police reports are as detailed as I like. The detective on the Martin case did a pretty decent job, but the file for Carson Pritchett leaves a lot to be desired. I did talk to the detective working the case for Steven Carlisle, and he remembers they found a letter in Carlisle's safe. It got taken into evidence, but when I called to see if they still had it, no one can seem to find it. The detective couldn't remember exactly what the letter said, but he did remember it had a Bible verse as the signature.

"I've also got the list Cole sent me of any major purchases of the high-gauge fencing wire and natural-fiber rope in Virginia and all the surrounding states, but it's got a couple thousand hits. All we can get from that is a time and date stamp and what store, and then we can match it with credit card purchases to find a name."

"I can go through Donnelly's case files from around the time of Carson Pritchett's murder to when the letter was sent to Donnelly with the Bible verse on it."

"Magnolia is already working on it, and she should have some useful information for us before too long. But in the meantime…" he said, coming to his feet, "…we need to get some sleep."

"I've been asleep," I said. "And now I'm wide awake." I looked down at my empty plate. "Hey, where'd the rest of my sandwich go?"

"You ate it," he said, coming around the desk and pulling me to my feet. He took the plate from my hand and set it in the chair.

"What are you up to, Lawson?" I asked as his hands crept inside my robe. I'd stopped thinking about food and work, and my breath caught as his thumb skimmed the underside of my breast. The pulse in my neck thrummed and my head fell back on its own accord as his hand trailed lower.

"I'm just trying to help you sleep," he said, kissing my neck.

"I hate to break it to you," I said, panting. "But you're not doing a very good job of it."

"Mmm," he said, lifting me slightly so I sat on the edge of the desk. My robe had disappeared somewhere along the way, and stars glittered behind my eyes as he stepped between my thighs.

"My bad," he whispered.

My eyes popped open a couple of hours later before the sun had a chance to rise, and I realized I had the rare treat of being awake before Jack. He slept on his back with nothing but the sheet barely covering his waist, and his arm was splayed above his head.

I got out of bed and felt around for my robe, and then remembered it had gotten left downstairs, so I pulled on a pair of sweats and made my way downstairs for coffee. I figured it was time to leave a cup for Jack to wake up to instead of the other way around.

I was feeling pretty proud of myself, and I wondered if the euphoria I felt this morning was how all morning people felt all the time, when Doug ruined it for me.

"Happy Halloween," he said, jumping out from behind the kitchen door wearing a Frankenstein mask.

I shrieked and threw the closest thing I could find, which happened to be my favorite coffee mug, and it bounced off Doug's forehead and then hit the floor, shattering into a thousand pieces.

"Told you," Carver said, rolling in behind him. "Bad idea."

"Ouch," Doug said, removing the mask and rubbing his forehead.

"You're lucky it wasn't a bullet," I said, going to the pantry to get the broom and dustpan. "Probably not the best idea to jump out at people in our line of work." I handed Doug the broom and dustpan and pointed to the floor.

"I told him that too," Carver said. "But sometimes you have to learn lessons the hard way. Where's Jack?"

"Still sleeping," I said. "He was up late. I don't want to disturb him. "

"Speaking of Halloween," Carver said.

"Were we?" I asked, making Carver smile.

"I hear there's a party tonight. I need to find a costume. What are you wearing?"

"A taser," I said. "In case anyone wants to make small talk." I poured two cups of coffee and doctored mine and left Jack's black the way he liked it.

"Looks like you two got a lot of work done last night," Carver said. "Magnolia is still compiling information, but it shouldn't be too long."

I felt the heat in my cheeks when he mentioned the work we'd been doing the night before. "I'm going to take this to Jack, and then I've got to get to the funeral home. We've got a full day ahead of us."

"Sure, sure," Carver said, and then he pulled something from his back to hand to me. "I thought you might want to take this back upstairs with you."

I grabbed my robe and ignored his laughter, only sloshing a little hot coffee on my hand as I fled the room.

Jack was awake when I got back upstairs, and I was a little bummed I missed out on seeing him wake up.

"You're up," I said, bringing him his coffee. He was sitting up against the headboard with the sheet over his waist, looking very, very good, and I looked at the clock to see how much time I had.

"Not enough," Jack said, reading my mind.

"I was hoping you'd be able to sleep longer," I said.

"I would have if World War III hadn't been going on downstairs."

"Doug jumped out at me with a mask on. It's Halloween."

"Hmmph," Jack said, and took a sip. "I guess he's lucky you didn't shoot him."

"That was pretty much my thought too. About the block party tonight—"

"Let me guess," he said. "You don't know if you'll be able to make it because things might be too busy at the funeral home."

"Well, it's true," I said defensively. "Things are busy."

"The entire town is shutting down at four o'clock today," he said. "You don't have any viewings scheduled. I even managed to find a costume for you to wear."

I narrowed my eyes. "When did you have time to find me a costume?"

"When I sent Officer Chen out yesterday during her lunch break to find you one."

I shook my head in disbelief. "As a taxpayer, I find your misuse of Officer Chen's time questionable."

Jack grinned. "She was on her lunch break, and she volunteered to do it because she knows how much you hate parties. So your taxpayer dollars are safe."

"I knew I never liked her," I said. "Just for that, when I take donuts by the station this morning, I'm going to make sure Chen doesn't get one."

"Does it help to know that Chen doesn't eat donuts?" Jack asked.

"A cop that doesn't eat donuts? I've never heard of such a thing."

"Why are you trying to make my cops fat?"

"Because I promised Tom Daly I'd stop by his donut shop this week, and I'm going to buy enough donuts to make sure he doesn't go out of business this month."

"You'll make them fat and get diabetes," he said, pulling off the sheet and getting out of bed.

I must have made a sound because Jack turned and looked at me, and then he smiled. "I really like being married to you."

"Maybe we could multitask in the shower again to save time. My back has mostly stopped hurting from the last time."

"There's only one problem," he said on the way to the shower.

"What's that?"

"You've got too many clothes on."

13

I WAS AN EXCELLENT MULTITASKER.

It was still early by the time I turned onto the square and headed toward the Donut Palace. It would've been smarter to park at the funeral home and walk there. The square was bedlam with everyone decorating and preparing for the block party. I ended up parking in front of the sheriff's office in a reserved spot, and walked the two blocks.

There was no line out the door at Tom's, but I was glad to see there were other customers inside.

"Hey, Doc," Tom said, his face lighting up when he saw me. "You made it."

"I told you I'd be in," I said.

"Heard y'all caught the John Donnelly murder," he said, and the other people who were sitting at the little two-tops enjoying their donuts quieted down so they could hear.

"We did," I told him. "Things have been busy. I'm going to need enough donuts for the entire sheriff's office."

"Oh, wow," he said, excitement gleaming in his eyes. "I've got a fresh batch just about ready to come out."

"Perfect," I said.

"I've always thought about doing an account service for the businesses in town, especially places like the fire department and the sheriff's office. I figure it wouldn't be too hard to set up a standing order a couple of times a week and have them delivered."

"I think that's a brilliant idea," I said. "You can count the funeral home as your first delivery client." And then I had another thought and tried to tell myself to stay out of it, but before I knew it my mouth was opening and words were coming out. "You know who would be great at helping you set things up is Emmy Lu," I told him. "She's a wonder with organization and filling orders." And she was single. Of course, Emmy Lu was older than Tom, but things like that didn't seem to matter nowadays.

"Really? That'd be great. Just tell her to stop by anytime. I haven't been this excited about the business in a long time. I thought for sure when Lady Jane's moved in that was it for us."

"No," I said, tamping down the guilt. "There's room in this town for the both of you."

I paid for the donuts and thanked him before I could tell any more lies or make any more matchmaking attempts. I hadn't really thought too far ahead what it was going to be like to carry six large bags of donuts two blocks to the sheriff's office. I still had a block to go when Martinez came up behind me.

"Doc, have I ever told you how you're my favorite person?" he asked.

"Really," I said, smiling. "And it's got nothing to do with the fact I'm hauling around a bunch of donuts."

"Those are donuts in those bags? No way," he said, looking shocked. "I thought maybe you'd gotten some new perfume or something. You've got stray dogs, and a couple of weird-looking dudes, that have been walking behind you for a while.

"Very funny," I said, taking one box out of a bag, and then passing the bags over to him. "Make sure you share those. And don't eat too many or you'll get a pooch over your duty belt."

"I've still got metabolism on my side," he said. "I've got a few years before I have to worry about a pooch. I figure that's when I'll know it's time to get married."

"Lucky girl," I said. "I've got to head out."

"Thanks for the donuts, Doc," he said. "See you at the party tonight."

I groaned and shook my head, and then made my way back to the Suburban. I got in and inhaled. I smelled delicious. No wonder stray dogs were following me.

It took me twenty minutes to get through traffic and past roadblocks and to the funeral home, and by the time I'd parked under the portico and walked into the kitchen, I'd sniffed myself so much I had a sugar high.

Everyone was gathered in the kitchen since we technically hadn't opened for business yet. Lily and Sheldon were sitting at the island drinking coffee, and Emmy Lu was frying eggs and telling a story about how her youngest put firecrackers under her bed when he was little and snuck in to light them when she was sleeping.

"It scared the daylights out of me. I couldn't hear, see, or think, and then the mattress caught on fire. Let's just say my youngest has more of his daddy in him than I'd like, but by the time I got through with him he couldn't sit for a week."

"I'm never having kids," Lily said.

"Oh, sugar," Emmy Lu said. "They're not all like that. It's mostly a lot of good times with the occasional splash of pure terror to keep things lively. You might change your mind one day."

"I don't think so," Lily said. "I enjoy my body, and I don't enjoy screaming babies or dirty diapers. What about you, Dr. Graves? Do you want kids?"

"Someday," I said, putting the box of donuts on the table.

"These aren't Lady Jane's," Sheldon said, eyeing the box like I'd plopped a litter box in the middle of the table.

"No, they're from the Donut Palace. We support all small businesses in this town. There's room for everyone."

"Except for the *Gazette*," Emmy Lu said. "I stopped my subscription to their paper when they got so nasty."

"And I don't shop at the Five and Dime anymore because I feel like it's false advertising," Sheldon said. "So I don't support them."

"I won't go to that new Italian place that bought that old house on Rosehill. The food was all right, but those guys are New York Italian. They'd scream at you if you didn't order fast enough, and one lady had so much anxiety she ran out crying."

"Good to know," I said, thinking I'd been wanting to try that place. "Oh, Emmy Lu. Tom Daly was thinking about starting a subscription delivery service for the businesses in town. I told him you might be able to help him get set up with the organizational side of things."

"Tom Daly," she said, her cheeks going pink. "He's a sweet fella. Always polite. And truth be told, I prefer his donuts to Lady Jane's. She's a little high handed with the sugar if you ask me."

"Good," I said. "He said just to stop by anytime. Do we have all the viewings and funerals scheduled for this week?"

"I just finished putting everything into the calendar and sending it to you," Emmy Lu said. "We haven't gotten any more calls from the hospital or other families, so I'm assuming the other four victims went somewhere else. Mrs. Lassiter asked for the viewing to be Wednesday night and the funeral on Thursday. That'll be enough time for an announcement to go in the paper for anyone who wants to attend, but she's in pretty rough shape and she didn't want it to drag out all week.

"Then we've got Lucy Randolph with a viewing Thursday night and the funeral on Friday. Stanley Turkus was sent off for cremation, so we'll just have the memorial service for him Friday evening. And then there's Kathleen Woodson. Her husband asked that we leave her in a viewing room all week so people can come and pay their respects, and then we'll do a marathon memorial service on Saturday and the funeral on Sunday afternoon. He wanted there to be plenty of time for their out-of-town friends and family to come in. He also bought the most expensive coffin and our premium package funeral service."

"Good," I said. "You'll all get paid this week. Anything else?"

"Don't forget we close at four today for the block party tonight," she said.

"Can't wait," Sheldon said. "I'm going as Howie from *The Big Bang Theory*. My mom found me an orange turtleneck and she sewed me this awesome NASA jacket. It looks just like the real ones."

"My boyfriend and I decided to go vintage," Lily said.

"Like Lucy and Desi?"

"Who's that?" she asked.

"Never mind." I took a donut out of the box and took a bite.

"I'm going as Monica Lewinsky," she said.

"And your boyfriend is going as Bill Clinton?" Emmy Lu asked.

"No, he's going as the cigar."

I choked on my donut, and that's when Jack came in.

"Must've been a good joke," he said. "Sorry I missed it."

I went to the fridge and got a bottle of water and drank half of it in one swallow. "What's up?" I asked.

"You should be good to release John Donnelly's body to his family," he said. "I don't think there's anything new we're going to learn from it."

"I can give next of kin a call if you'd like," Lily said.

"Call Michael Donnelly," I said, digging in my bag for his card with his number on it. "That's his son."

"Do you think they'll do the funeral here?"

"Doubtful," I said. "Donnelly's practice was in King George Proper, and most of his associates and friends live in that area. They'll probably use the Here and Now."

Lily made a face. "John Luke has a heavy hand with makeup. And I heard a rumor he doesn't dress his deceased in underpants after he does the embalming. I bet he has a big drawer of stolen underpants."

"I went to school with a girl who stole people's underpants," Sheldon broke in. "She'd sneak in the boys' locker room, steal them, and then she'd run them right up the flagpole."

Lily patted Sheldon on the back as they walked out of the room and I heard her ask. "Did she do that to everyone's underpants or just yours?"

"On that pleasant note," Emmy Lu said. "I'm going to head back to my desk. We'll get everyone laid out in the viewing rooms this morning and make sure everything is all set."

"Thanks, Emmy Lu," I said and then I looked at Jack. "What's up? I didn't think I'd see you again so soon. Or do you want to give my office shower a go?"

"Not unless you're trying to paralyze me," he said. "You didn't happen to take out another insurance policy on me, did you?"

"Hey, if you can't hang just let me know."

Jack's eye narrowed. "If I didn't have something important to tell you I'd show you exactly how much I can hang."

"Promises, promises," I said.

"You're a handful," he said.

"Thank you."

"It wasn't a compliment."

"Of course it was," I told him. "Otherwise you'd be bored to tears. Now, what's up?"

"The data Magnolia was compiling came through not long after you left. It didn't take long to start putting things together. Check this out," he said, taking two stacks of paper out of his bag. "First we've got the bulk orders of fencing wire and natural-fiber rope. Then we've got Donnelly's case files. Guess whose name shows up in Donnelly's files as a plaintiff in a class action lawsuit against Carson Pritchett and Steven Carlisle, and whose name also shows up on a credit card receipt for a bulk order of fencing wire and rope?"

"I have no idea," I said. "Who?"

He flipped through each stack until I saw a name circled in red on each one. "Magnolia saved us a lot of time on this one with the fencing order. But Carver and I started going through the case files this morning after you left and this case was within the right time frame."

"Wow," I said, staring at the name. "I can't believe it. What do you want to do?"

"I think we need to take another trip out to the crime scene," he said.

14

I DIDN'T KNOW HOW I FELT ABOUT THE NEWS JACK had just delivered. Relieved to know who was responsible, certainly. But I also found I had a great deal of remorse. It was a sad situation all around, but the truth was four people were dead, and someone needed to pay for those crimes, no matter the reasoning behind them.

I noticed there was still crime scene tape roping off the area where John Donnelly's body had been found, and the scarecrow pole was back in the hole, but it looked like a plain metal cross without a body on it.

Jack parked in the middle of the one-way road, and then he bent down to check his backup weapon in his ankle holster. It was the only thing that saved his life. A shot rang out and shattered the front windshield of the Tahoe and buried itself in the headrest of Jack's seat.

I ducked down in my seat automatically, but I didn't know how much good it did if the shooter was at an elevation where he could see inside the car. I didn't have to think much more about it, because Jack threw open his door, grabbed me by the shirt, and pulled me across the seat and onto the ground so we were hidden behind the Tahoe.

"Backup is not too far behind us," he said. "We were waiting on a warrant to search the property, but Cole has it in hand." Jack took out his weapon and checked the magazine. "Stay down low," he told me. He crept up slowly and reached an arm into the Tahoe for his radio so he could call dispatch and another shot rang out.

"Oh, God," I said, tugging at the back of his shirt. "Just wait for backup."

"I was calling for backup," he said. "I don't want them driving into live fire." He moved quickly and grabbed the radio before crouching down beside me again and called it in to dispatch. "Shots fired," Jack said, and then he gave the address. "Alert Cole and any other officers heading out to the Cotton farm. He's armed and dangerous."

"10-4," dispatch said back. "Keep the line open."

"Donald Cotton," Jack yelled. "You're only making things worse."

"Not from where I'm standing," Cotton yelled back. "You don't understand."

"Sure I do," Jack said. "I read your wife's medical file. She gets hit by a car in a freak accident and breaks her leg bad in a couple of places. Dr. Carlisle decides she needs a bone graft. Only he's working with Carson Pritchett, who has a history of black market medical practices, but they're both making a fortune, so Carlisle didn't really care where the donors came from. But this was Pritchett's first time with organ donation, and he didn't realize one of the patients he'd harvested from had an aggressive form of cancer. So when he did the bone graft on your wife, Amy, he basically sentenced her to death. He did the same thing to seven other people."

"Then you know they all got what they deserved," Cotton said.

"You can't take matters into your own hands," Jack said. "That doesn't make you any better than the people who killed your wife."

"It sure as hell makes me feel better," he said.

Jack was scooting forward toward the front of the Tahoe. "I think he's on the roof of his house," Jack whispered.

"What about Dana Martin?" Jack called out. "She had two little kids who no longer have a mother."

"She should have thought about that before she lied to cover for Carlisle. They were sleeping together, you know. And when it came time for the trial she got on the stand and swore that they had no knowledge of where the donors came from, even though there was evidence that Pritchett and Carlisle had both deposited hefty payments into hidden accounts. But just like smoke, all that information disappeared when John Donnelly took the case so those bastards would walk free. You think justice in this country is for everyone? That's naïve. Because men like John Donnelly don't believe in justice. They believe in money. And every one of those people killed, and then they lied and smirked their way through that farce of a trial. And I and the other families who'd lost their loved ones were left with nothing but attorney fees. Where's the justice in that?"

"None of those other families decided to become killers," Jack said. I could hear the sirens screaming down the county road, and then they turned and were headed toward us and I breathed out a sigh of relief. It would all be over soon.

"I did what I had to do," Cotton said. "I have no regrets. They all betrayed their oath to their professions. Their lives became forfeit the second the last handful of dirt was thrown onto Amy's coffin."

"Come down, Donald," Jack said. "Believe it or not, I do understand why you did what you did. It was wrong. But I understand it. Come down and talk to me. We can get you help."

"I don't need help," he said. "I didn't think you'd suspect me if the body was found on my own property."

"We didn't," Jack said. "That was very clever."

"But I knew you'd figured it out when I saw you coming today. I realized all you'd have to do is look through Donnelly's files to find my name."

"We found the letter you sent him six years ago," Jack said. "With the Bible verse."

"I was going to be a preacher," he said. "Did you know that? Before I bought the farm. It seemed like poetic justice. An eye for an eye, right?"

"How about thou shall not murder?" Jack asked.

"There's a fine line between righteous justice and murder in my book. Just look at the death penalty."

"How about if I come to you," Jack said. "We can talk for as long as you want."

"No," I hissed. "Are you crazy?"

Jack held up a finger to shush me, and I bit my tongue. But boy, did I have a lot I was going to say to him when this was over.

"I'm coming out," Jack said. "If you shoot, things are not going to end the way you want them to."

"Sorry, Sheriff," Cotton said. "But things are ending exactly the way I want them to."

"No," Jack said just as a shot rang out, and he crawled low until he could see, and then he stood to his feet and started running.

I was right behind him, but Cotton's lifeless body rolled from the roof and hit with a thud on the ground. There was nothing any of us could do, and I thanked God there was only one casualty to speak of. Things could've been much worse.

My breath heaved and my hands shook as I reached for Jack. Other officers had come running behind us and they were checking Cotton's pulse, but I just had to hold on for a second. I kept replaying the first shot coming through the car window, and it had only been luck that had kept Jack from getting hit. In the blink of an eye…that's all it took for a life to end.

"Please don't ever volunteer to sacrifice yourself to a murderer again," I said, squeezing him tight. "Because I can promise you I'll be the one threatening your life next time."

Jack chuckled and buried his face in the side of my neck and breathed in. "Why do you smell like donuts?"

"Because I eat so much of them it's what I secrete," I said sarcastically. "You're bleeding." I moved his head to see where the blood was coming from.

"Just glass," he said. "I just need a Band-Aid."

"If I give you a Band-Aid do we still have to go to the Halloween party tonight? We could stay in and work off the adrenaline instead."

"Nice try," he said. "But don't forget we've got an election in a couple of weeks. We need to see and be seen. But if you come to the party tonight, I promise

I'll take the day off tomorrow and we can stay in bed all day."

"Deal," I said. "But maybe tell Carver and Doug to go home. I don't want to stay in bed *all* day. You do your best work in the kitchen."

Jack threw his head back and laughed. Everything was going to be okay.

EPILOGUE

Jack had been right, as usual. Going to the Halloween block party on the square hadn't killed me. He'd also been right about the costume. Chen had bought me a horse's head that had eyes that looked like it belonged to a meth-head and a pair of brown leggings and a matching oversized sweatshirt. I'd hardly had to talk to anyone while I was wearing the head, but it seemed to freak little kids out and it was hot in there, so I eventually took it off, made small talk, and drank free beer. All in all, it was a great night.

The morning was already off to a good start. Carver and Doug had packed their bags and headed out bright and early, and as promised, Jack had taken the day off and was in the shower. I'd told Emmy Lu to call me if I was needed, but there was nothing on the schedule today they couldn't handle. It was just the two of us for a solid twenty-four hours. And I had plans. Big plans.

I figured the best way to stop secreting donuts was to lower my intake, so I made some toast while I was waiting on the coffee. And then I decided toast probably wasn't going to cut it, so I got out the frying pan and decided to try my hand at French toast again. I wanted to make sure Jack had plenty of energy.

My phone buzzed, and I checked it, only to see a blocked number, so I sent it straight to voicemail. I'd barely taken a step away when the phone buzzed again, and this time a number showed but it was one I didn't recognize. I frowned and sent the call to voicemail again. In Jack's line of work and the media coverage we'd gotten over the last year, I didn't give my cell number out to just anyone.

I scrambled the eggs and let the bread soak in the yolks before I remembered I'd forgotten the butter and I hadn't turned on the pan. There was something in my gut that was stirring, and worry set in when my phone started buzzing again. I heard Jack's footsteps on the stairs at the same time I heard a car door slam from the driveway. And then another door slammed. I looked out the window in time to see Carrie Colson check her hair once in the side-view mirror and grab a microphone.

"Why are there reporters in our driveway?" I asked Jack when he came in the kitchen. I'd never seen the look on his face before. His skin color was ashen and there was a banked fury inside of him that made his black eyes glitter with rage. He was holding on to his temper by a thread.

My phone buzzed again. "It keeps doing that," I said. "What's going on? Jack, you're scaring me. Is someone hurt?"

"No, no one is hurt," he said. His voice was different. It was thin and raspy.

"One of the guys emailed me the paper's headline this morning," he said, putting his phone on the counter so I could read it.

My blood ran cold.

Sheriff's Affair Results In Child He Abandoned

My gaze went to the author of the article and saw Floyd Parker's name, and then I quickly read the story. A story I knew to be true, down to the very last detail. Floyd hadn't missed a thing.

It's not something I'd thought about in a long time. There was no reason to. We'd all been young and stupid once upon a time, and everyone had a past. It's just that some pasts were better kept secrets than others. I knew this from experience.

Jack had been nineteen and a sophomore in college. He'd been infatuated with this woman—Amber something—who'd been twenty-three and newly married. She'd been a kindergarten teacher of all things.

One thing had led to another and they'd had a fast and furious affair that had lasted a few weeks before it had fizzled. She'd been scared her husband was going to find out and put a stop to things, and Jack had never let himself get attached to a woman because, in those days, he'd been bound and determined to try them all to see which one fit the best. So he'd shrugged her off and gone his own way with no love lost either way.

Until she'd let him know she was pregnant. I remember the night he showed up at my dorm room, his face pale and showing all the symptoms of shock. He'd been scared to death, and there'd been no plans in his life to start a family that young. He was even more scared that his dad was going to kill him. Mr. Lawson was a good man, but boy, could he put the fear of God in a person.

I'd held him when he'd cried, and supported him when he'd decided he'd do whatever it took to be a good father. And he would've been a good father. *Will* be a good father. Someday. But Amber had come back after her initial panic had subsided and told Jack she wanted him out of her life completely. She didn't want him to be part of the baby's life. She wanted her husband to think the baby was his, and had lied about the baby's due date so it coincided with the last time they'd been together. And she begged Jack not to make trouble for them. She told him her husband would make all their lives miserable if he did.

Jack hadn't really had much choice in the matter. So he'd agreed, and then he'd sworn me to secrecy. I knew he'd regretted coming to my dorm room and letting me see him at his most vulnerable. But he also knew he could trust me. He'd decided the whole thing had never happened, and he suggested I forget about it too. It was the only thing we could do.

"I don't understand," I said. "Why? How?"

"You're the only person who knows the truth that's written in that paper. I never told another person."

I shook my head involuntarily, trying to get my brain to understand what he was implying.

"What are you saying? You think I told Floyd about this?"

"You two used to be involved," he said. His cop face was firmly in place, and his posture was so stiff I thought he might break.

"We didn't used to be involved," I said, the blood rushing in my ears. My skin was on fire with dread. "We had one night of lousy sex. Discussing my best friend's secrets over pillow talk isn't exactly my MO."

"The proof is in black and white," he said. "There's nothing that can be done about it now. I've already gotten calls asking for my resignation."

"There's nothing to be done?" I asked, my voice getting louder. "You're going to stand there and accuse me of betraying you when you know I'd rather die than hurt you in any way, and you say there's nothing to be done?"

Jack shrugged. "Floyd bided his time. He's held on to this information for years until he could use it at the right moment. It's game, set, and match for him."

"I don't give a damn about the election or Floyd Parker. All I care about right here, right now, is whether or not you believe me when I tell you I was not the person who gave Floyd Parker that story."

Jack looked at me, and I saw the disappointment in his eyes along with the acceptance. "I think you'd never do anything purposely to hurt me."

"But by accident?" I asked, wanting to make sure I was crystal clear in my understanding.

"I think things happen in the heat of the moment. Even inadvertently. Maybe you didn't even realize how much information you gave him. It could've been just enough for him to start digging."

My eyes burned, but I didn't think I could cry. It felt as if something was pressing against my chest, and I was having trouble catching a breath.

"You don't believe me," I said, feeling hollow inside.

"Accidents happen, and facts are facts. You and I are the only people who knew about this."

"Right," I said, pushing his phone back across the counter. I didn't want to see any more. My phone was buzzing again, but now I knew why. "Well, at least I know where I stand."

"All we can do is damage control at this point," he said. "A place like King George County still cares about the morality of its leaders." His voice was even and empty, and I knew he was hurting. But I didn't care at the moment.

My own hurt was so consuming I wanted to curl up into a ball on the floor and rock the pain away. I wanted to scream.

I looked around the kitchen as if I were seeing it for the first time, and then I looked once more at Jack. He was staring out the window into the trees, lost in his own pain. I walked out of the kitchen and upstairs to the third-floor bedroom we'd shared for the last few months of our marriage.

I tried not to breathe in the scent of him as I went into the closet and started pulling clothes from the hangers. It didn't matter. None of it had ever mattered. I shoved everything I could fit into the old gray suitcase that had been mine before we'd married, and then I picked it up with a strength I hadn't realized I possessed and carried it down the stairs.

I didn't say goodbye. I didn't stop to get my phone. I just walked out. I walked through the reporters gathered on our lawn and to the Suburban, and I didn't care if I backed over anyone who got in my way as I sped down the driveway.

I realized my father had only ever told one truth my entire life, and I didn't know why I was thinking of him now, here in this moment, when my life was crumbling at my feet. But his only truth had been to say that the only person you could ever count on in life was yourself.

Even the people you'd die for could turn on you in an instant.

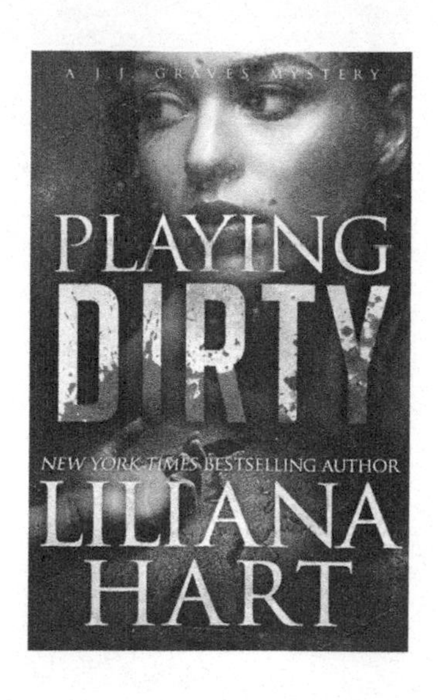

J.J. Graves and her husband, Sheriff Jack Lawson, are sworn to protect and serve. But with a secret out in the open and the election all but lost, J.J. and Jack have to figure out how to work together while their marriage is torn apart. Because death doesn't stop for anyone.

Coming December 1, 2020! Preorder Today!

ABOUT THE AUTHOR

Liliana Hart is a *New York Times*, *USA Today*, and Publisher's Weekly bestselling author of more than sixty titles. After starting her first novel her freshman year of college, she immediately became addicted to writing and knew she'd found what she was meant to do with her life. She has no idea why she majored in music.

Since publishing in June 2011, Liliana has sold more than six-million books. All three of her series have made multiple appearances on the *New York Times* list.

Liliana can almost always be found at her computer writing, hauling five kids to various activities, or spending time with her husband. She calls Texas home.

If you enjoyed reading this, I would appreciate it if you would help others enjoy this book, too.

Recommend it. Please help other readers find this book by recommending it to friends, readers' groups and discussion boards.

Review it. Please tell other readers why you liked this book by reviewing.

Connect with me online:
www.lilianahart.com

facebook.com/LilianaHart
instagram.com/LilianaHart
bookbub.com/authors/liliana-hart

ALSO BY LILIANA HART

JJ Graves Mystery Series

Dirty Little Secrets

A Dirty Shame

Dirty Rotten Scoundrel

Down and Dirty

Dirty Deeds

Dirty Laundry

Dirty Money

A Dirty Job

Dirty Devil

Playing Dirty

The MacKenzies of Montana

Dane's Return

Thomas's Vow

Riley's Sanctuary

Cooper's Promise

Grant's Christmas Wish

Jayden's Hope

The MacKenzies Boxset

MacKenzie Security Series

Seduction and Sapphires

Shadows and Silk

Secrets and Satin

Sins and Scarlet Lace

Sizzle

Crave

Scorch

MacKenzie Security Omnibus 1

MacKenzie Security Omnibus 2

Lawmen of Surrender (MacKenzies-1001 Dark Nights)

1001 Dark Nights: Captured in Surrender

1001 Dark Nights: The Promise of Surrender

1001 Dark Nights: Sweet Surrender

1001 Dark Nights: Dawn of Surrender

The MacKenzie World (read in any order)

Trouble Maker

Bullet Proof

Deep Trouble

Delta Rescue

Desire and Ice

Rush

Spies and Stilettos

Wicked Hot

Hot Witness

Avenged

Never Surrender

Addison Holmes Mystery Series

Whiskey Rebellion

Whiskey Sour

Whiskey For Breakfast

Whiskey, You're The Devil

Whiskey on the Rocks

Whiskey Tango Foxtrot

Whiskey and Gunpowder

The Gravediggers

The Darkest Corner

Gone to Dust

Say No More

Stand Alone Titles

Breath of Fire

Kill Shot

Catch Me If You Can

All About Eve

Paradise Disguised

Island Home

The Witching Hour

Books by Liliana Hart and Scott Silverii

The Harley and Davidson Mystery Series

The Farmer's Slaughter

A Tisket a Casket

I Saw Mommy Killing Santa Claus

Get Your Murder Running

Deceased and Desist

Malice In Wonderland

Tequila Mockingbird

Gone With the Sin

Made in the USA
Las Vegas, NV
11 February 2021

17669783R10173